ANGEL BABIES

CLIVE ALANDO TAYLOR

authorHOUSE®

AuthorHouse™ UK Ltd.
500 Avebury Boulevard
Central Milton Keynes, MK9 2BE
www.authorhouse.co.uk
Phone: 08001974150

Published by AuthorHouse 3/07/2012

ISBN: 978-1-4678-9001-4 (sc)
ISBN: 978-1-4678-9002-1 (e)

SYNOPSIS

It was very much my intention not to state the name of any particular place in the script as I thought that the telling of the story of the Angel Babies is in itself about believing in who you are, and also about facing up to your fears. The Angel Babies is also set loosely in accordance with the foretelling of the Bibles Revelations. I thought it would be best to take this approach, as the writing of the script is also about the Who, What, Where, When, How and Why scenario that we all often deal with in our ongoing existence. It would also not be fair to myself or to anyone else who has read the Angel Babies to not acknowledge this line of questioning, for instance, who are we? What are we doing here? Where did we come from? And when will our true purpose be known? And how do we fulfil our true potential to better ourselves and others, the point of which are the statements that I am also making in the Angel Babies and about Angels in particular, Is that if we reach far into our minds we still wonder Where did the Angels come from and what is their place in this world. I know sometimes that we all wish and pray for the miracle of life to reveal itself but the answer to this mystery truly lives within us and around us, I only hope that you will find the Angel Babies an interesting narrative and exciting story as I have had in bringing it to life, after all there could be an Angel Baby being born right now.

INSPIRIT ★ ASPIRE ★ ESPRIT ★ INSPIRE

CONTENTS

ANGEL BABIES
SELAH I

Ext: Its' Daytime and Selah is praying by a circular gravestone outside an old and abandoned burial ground, which is overlooked by a dilapidated ageing church. She is kneeling down by the side of a gravestone that is engraved with the words GOD'S STONE. Selah is pregnant and her waters are about to break.

SELAH

Ext: She couples her hands together to pray.

And I will praise god in his sanctuary

Ext: Selah looks to the sky

And I will praise him in his mighty firmament,
and I will praise him for his mighty acts

Ext: She pauses for breath as she feels the pain of her contractions, as she slumps by the gravestone.

And I will praise him according to his excellent greatness! And I shall praise him with the sound of the trumpet, and I will praise him with the lute and harp!

And I will praise him with stringed instruments and flutes, and I shall praise him with clashing cymbals!

Ext: **Again Selah pauses and looks around and about her, from the ground on which she kneels to pray to the heavens above her.**

Selah

So let everything that breathes praise the lord

Ext: **Just then Selah slumps to the ground surrounded by the beating of her own heart, and the gasping of air for her own breath to breathe, as each moment of her life edges away. Although it is daytime, the sky is a dark misty grey and filled with an eerie and cold feeling as the rains begin to fall down about her, weakening, faint and tired body.**

Ext: **Suddenly during her prayer, Selah is surprised to hear a very familiar voice coming from behind her. It is the voice of her beloved Hark, but he is not visible to her although as only an angelic shadow towers over the gravestone where she is now kneeling.**

Hark The Herald Angel

Don't despair my darling Selah, faith is having hope in all things that live and breathe in the oneness of God…!

Selah

…HARK!

The Beginning

ANGEL BABIES

SELAH II

Time is neither here or there, it is a time in between time as it is the beginning and yet the end of time. This is a story of the Alpha and the Omega, the first and the last and yet as we enter into this revelation, we begin to witness the birth of the Angel Babies a time of heavenly conception when dying Angels gave birth to Angelic children who were born to represent the order of the new world. The names of these Angel Babies remained unknown but they carried the Seal of their fathers written on their foreheads, and in all it totalled one hundred and forty four thousand Angels and this is the story of one of them.

Angel Simeon

Sound the horn of the trumpeters as a sign to let it be known
that this day in the heavens that his son has been born

Pablo the Immortal

And what word of the Earth Mother Selah, Simeon?

Angel Simeon

I'm afraid I have grave news to pass onto you this day,
the Earth Mother Selah, has died while giving birth,
the spiritual body has left the physical form after the
deliverance of the child and is now residing in the
soul cages, my only fear is for the metaphysical change

of the new born infant, once he reaches adulthood, all
that is left of the Earth Mother is her mortal body

Pablo the Immortal

And the new born infant Simeon, what will become of his
livelihood, what say we to Hark the Herald Angel?

Angel Simeon

He will be fine Pablo, after all he has us to
watch over him until his appointed time

Pablo the Immortal

Then I will commence your bidding, the horns of
the trumpeters will be sounded in the heavens

Int: Meanwhile Selah's body is being monitored in a hospital.

Dr

I'm afraid there were some complications, we've lost
the responses of the mother, in my attempt to revive
her she became unconscious, this happened as a result
of fits and seizures during the delivery which led
to a cardiac arrest, we tried everything to revive
her but there was no response what so ever

Nurse

Its' been a difficult time for you Dr, your not to take
things so harshly, you tried your best, I'm sorry that she
didn't pull through and that poor child its' a shame, now
we'll have to inform welfare of the present situation, I do
believe she was a single parent or she would have been if she
hadn't of… well you know, should I make a report of all that
took place in the delivery room and have it on your desk

Dr

Nurse, I want the baby looked after in the intensive care
unit and just follow normal procedure, tell the welfare
assessment team we'll be in touch with a report to follow,
we have far too many babies at risk anyway, if he's fit and
healthy then we should be able to pass on his care to them

Int: **The Nurse carries the child off to the baby care unit and leaves him there unsupervised for a moment, as the child lay peacefully on his bed, the room became filled with a cold chilling air and then suddenly Angel Simeon appears standing over the new born infant.**

Angel Simeon

Your Father is a great Angel, almost a Saint of an Angel, we weren't sure if you were going to make it but you did, you will be fit and healthy and strong all the days of your life, there will be much for you to do at your appointed time of life, you shall fly the like Eagle and you shall be more delicate than the Butterfly, your song will topple mountains and sway the rivers into oceans and you shall soar the skies and reach great heights, but this I tell you as a blessing you are the least of our kind and there is one among us who will try to destroy you and those who are of us, I am here as your guardian and I have with me the Seal of your father which I shall put upon you this very day and when it is removed in time you shall know what it means to be an Angel

Int: **Angel Simeon put his hand on the head of the child for a second, and then removed it, the child seemed to smile at him for a while and still remained quite peaceful as he lay on his bed, then once again the room became empty and Angel Simeon was seen no more.**

Int: **Somewhere in the realms of the Empyrean Pablo the Immortal and Simeon are mediating.**

Pablo the Immortal

Simeon it will be well noted that you are fast approaching the last eclipse of your present time spell, if you don't put aside your present duties as Herald Angel then the chances of consummation and conception with an Earth Mother will be jeopardise, all of those of the first harvest, those with whom you fought have already sealed their covenants

Angel Simeon

We are old and somewhat use to our ways Pablo, we have seen many rotations of the Earth and its' existence, this is the sole purpose of our being, to be as watchers over our domain and to deliver it unto its' inheritance, yes you are right, it is true time has elapsed and I thank you for your concern but my thoughts are upon a certain Angel of our time, a certain saint of an Angel

Pablo the Immortal
You mean Angel Hark

Angel Simeon
Yes Hark, once he fought with me during the very first harvest, It was something that my whole life was prepared for, and this was also the last time he was to convey to me his deepest wishes to me, a promise of his covenant before his time spell ended, I was to ensure that his lifeblood would go on to maintain all that took place leading up to this very day, you know it's' funny Pablo, that to safeguard our own existence, how we must be unprepared for it and the forthcoming revelation which is yet unrealised, well what I am really trying to say Pablo is that I wish for you to allow me more time, until I am quite certain that our new born child is completely out of danger, I know that Angel Hark would want me to be his son's guardian until he has reached maturity

Int: A few months had passed and a young couple, a Mr Robert and his wife Chelle Stiles had previously registered themselves with a fostering and adoption agency. Their names had been put forward from the welfare officers working in their locality. Robert and Chelle Stiles were now due to see the baby infant at the hospital with which they had been granted access to visit, they entered the hospital with great expectation and in somewhat of a nervous state, the nurse was there to greet them.

Nurse
Mr and Mrs Stiles, could you please come this way, we have been expecting you, even thou you are a little bit early, I suppose your very eager to see the baby, well I can tell you that he is very much in good health and is cared for around the clock, by myself and the other staff nurses on duty, in the baby care unit

Mrs Stiles

Oh he's beautiful, look Robert he looks just like an angel lying there, and he's so tiny, can I hold him?

Nurse

Go ahead, you can pick him up if you want too, after all if you and Mr Stiles both don't mind, we've already spoken to the team at the welfare office and they have agreed with our senior Doctors that you and your husband are quite a suitable couple to have the child for adoption, so you'll be able to take him home as soon as possible

Mr Stiles

You mean to tell me that the fostering and adoption agency has already agreed to us having this child, well I must say that comes as a bit of a surprise, I thought it would take forever, I'm absolutely thrilled, my wife was so worried that we wouldn't fulfil the criteria, so he can really come home with us

Nurse

Yes!

Mr Stiles

Oh we didn't know

Mrs Stiles

No, Not at all, we weren't sure of anything

Mr Stiles

Anyway we will be more than happy to have this little chappie on board

Mrs Stiles

Baby! Robert, he's a baby, not a chappie

Nurse

So have you thought of a name yet?

Mr Stiles

A name now there's a thing

Mrs Stiles

He's not a thing Robert, I keep telling you, he's a baby and
he's ours, I won't have you suggesting he's anything else

Mr Stiles

Ok Chelle, I got the message, no need to be so sensitive,
so what do you suggest we call him, I mean the baby,
what do you think we should call the baby?

Mrs Stiles

I'm not sure, I can only think of girl's names, like Stephanie

Mr Stiles

You can't call a boy Stephanie

Mrs Stiles

What about Steven?

Mr Stiles

No! Not Steven, I've already got a cousin called Steven,
and I don't want to think or even discover that our baby
would turnout like him, a bloody drunken bum, low life, I
don't want any son of mine amounting to a complete nothing

Mrs Stiles

I know Robert, what if we put the two names together
and make one, ya know like Stephanie and Steven
and you get Stefan, well what do you think?

Mr Stiles

Stefan, Stefan Stiles, that's not bad Chelle, Stefan
Stiles, its' almost brilliant, yes the more I say it,
the more I like it, Stefan, now there's a thing

Nurse

So you've agreed then Mr and Mrs Stiles?

Mrs Stiles

Yes we have

Nurse

Ok Then, I'll just take you to our baby care offices
where you will have to sign some release forms, you
will also be given a month's supply of baby clothes and
food vouchers, this will also include blankets, feeding
bottles and sterilisers, so if you please follow me

Mrs Stiles

Oh Robert, I'm so happy about it all, we're really parents now
at last, its' so funny, I thought it would never happen, do
you think I'll make a good mother, I mean after all I don't
have much experience in motherhood, what with new babies,
well what do you think, did we make the right decision, I
mean there's so much in front of us now, the future, its'
all quite worrying, I mean really what will I do if he gets
sick or something, I mean little children their so fragile,
and they need to be breast fed you know and I don't have
any milk in my breast, he might suffer at such an early
age, I can't just raise him on that bottled stuff, its' all
artificial ya know, he might develop an allergy or something

Mr Stiles

Look just calm down Chelle, your getting yourself all worked
up about nothing, since we've arrived at the hospital you've
been in a right state, everything will be fine, the staff have
assured us he's in perfect health and they wouldn't turn him
over to us if he had something wrong with him, now would they?

Mrs Stiles

No I guess not, I'm just worried, that's all

Mr Stiles

Ok I understand but I'm sure that everything will
work out just fine and I can tell you now that
I'm not exactly prepared for fatherhood either
but I'm willing to give it a try if you are

9

Mrs Stiles
Of course I am silly

Ext: After the release forms were presented to Mr and Mrs Stiles, they gathered all of the baby's belongings together and loaded everything into their car. Both Robert and Chelle Stiles were quite excited and happy as their car pulled away out of the hospital grounds. The child was tucked away in his blankets and held in the arms of Mrs Stiles, they were now a family and a new life had begun for the three of them.

Int: Many years had passed by since Robert and Chelle Stiles first adopted their young baby boy Stefan and they had provided him with a loving home and all the care and attention that a mother and father could bestow upon a young child. Stefan had won their affections and had everything of a boy his age needed, he would sometimes play in the yard outdoors, or he would sometimes sit and think endlessly in his bedroom about life, and with this feeling came the realisation of a child that was now aware that he himself was becoming of age. All these signs worried Robert and Chelle Stiles, as they were not sure when would be the right time to tell him that they were indeed his adoptive parents and not his real ones, or whether they should reveal that his real mother died in circumstances none of which they really knew much about.

Int: The staff at the hospital revealed very little if anything at all about Stefan's real mother, Selah, as they thought for safety reasons it would be best left alone, the hospital only told the Stiles what they thought they needed to know, and Stefan had already had a taste of good family living, and if this was to be disrupted by him finding out about the truth, then it could result in a rebellious breakdown, which the Stiles wanted to avoid at any cost. Stefan had already completed junior school and it was the end of the holidays so he would soon be enrolling for college.

Int: Stefan was quite bright and fairly intelligent for his age and his scores in school in most of his classes were always just about average. It was the beginning of the new term and Robert and Chelle Stiles drove up to the front gate of Eastmore High School, Stefan got out of the car, and he was feeling anxious and eager and nervous as he took a glimpse at the new beginnings that stood between him and the double doors he now faced, he said goodbye to his parents and then slowly walked through the corridors that led to the great hall where the head principal was giving a welcoming talk to first year students as well as former students who had opted to stay on for a further year. Stefan arrived late but unnoticed by the majority of students and staff, except for one boy who was also just entering the great hallway of Eastmore High.

Head Principal

Well there you have it, its' been a good academic year for most of you but as for some, well I say some of you, I mean a few of you, if you are going on to become high achievers you will have to pass the end of this year's summer exams, and those of you retaking last year's exams, well you may take your leave now from the great hall and in the meantime I would like to take the opportunity to welcome those of you who are new to Eastmore High, its' quite simple really, at this school all you have to do is follow the rules and don't play the fool, we expect only the best from you as we provide you with the best facilities for the best education that get the best results, you will all be put in to class groups by the Senior Head Tutors, and so once you have heard your name called, please go and stand in line behind that teacher, Mrs Cooper you will be first

Mrs Cooper

Ok everyone, once you've heard me call your name, please go and stand in line behind that tutor, Mrs Green's class is as follows…

Bernadette Burns
Christine Hill
Julie Reid
Josephine Young
Jaspa Alal
Michael Casey
Benjamin Levi

Stefan Stiles

Int: Stefan and Jaspa start talking between themselves.

Jaspa Alal

Hey how you doin' man?

Stefan Stiles

I'm Ok I suppose, a bit nervous

Jaspa Alal

Yeah me too

Stefan Stiles

So what's your name?

Jaspa Alal

My names Jaspa, Jaspa Alal I'm Anglo Indian,
my mother is from India and my father is from
here, so what about you where you from?

Stefan Stiles

Well my name is Stefan and my parents are originally from
England, but I was born here, hey my parents are pretty cool
people but my mother goes on a bit, you know the usual stuff"

Jaspa Alal

Looks like we're in the same class together, it should be fun

**Int: The students all stood in line behind Mrs Green, who in
turn walked up to the great hall corridors and headed
towards the classrooms, Stefan walked at the back of the
line and as they entered into the classroom he sat himself
next to Jaspa.**

Mrs Green checked her register to see that everyone was present,
Stefan looked around the room which seemed to be quite large
inside and filled with maps and notice boards and the seats upon

which they sat were on platforms coming downward as if they were seated in a theatre.

The windows were wide and elongated with blinds rolled up to let in the rays of sunshine, for a moment he was blinded by a stream of sunlight and he quickly looked away, he then caught sight of a pair of eyes staring right at him, it was one of the girls in the classroom. She sat in the front row and was also taking the opportunity to explore the classroom in which they had entered, they both looked at each other only for a moment and although to Stefan it seemed to be forever.

Mrs Green finished her checking of the register and allowed the students sometime to go out into the school grounds to have a look around. Outside a man stood in the doorway that led to the school playing grounds, no one seemed to be bothered to take any notice of the tall distinguished man, who may very well have been a tutor himself, as they sat and talked for a little while the alarms sounded for the student to return to class, Jaspa and Stefan came rushing through the doors almost knocking the man to the ground, just then Stefan's books fell from his hands to the floor but Jaspa kept on running and left Stefan to deal with the mess.

Angel Simeon
Here let me help you with that, you seem to be hurry

Stefan Stiles
Oh no, that's no trouble, I can pick them up

Angel Simeon
No really, its' no trouble and in any case, if I
don't help you, you'll be late for your class

Stefan Stiles
So what are you hanging around here for
do you work here or something?

Angel Simeon
Well not exactly, I'm really here as a favour for a friend
of mine, he asked me to drop by and keep an eye on his son,
you could say its' just a passing visit as I was in town

Stefan Stiles

So what's this kid's name, maybe I can tell
him you were here looking for him?

Angel Simeon

Oh that won't be necessary, I've already seen him,
I was just checking to see if he was fitting in
O.k. but I can see that things are just fine

Stefan Stiles

Well whatever you say

Int: Stefan looked deeply at Angel Simeon who appeared to be a
warm and pleasant man, there also seemed to be a certain
aura in his presence that almost hypnotised Stefan. Angel
Simeon handed back some of the fallen books to Stefan
but as he did this, he discretely slipped and placed a
rather slim piece of paper with something written on, in
between Stefan's books, this slight of hand movement had
gone unnoticed by Stefan who at this point had everything
under control, so he took his books and started to walk
down the corridor.

Stefan walked into the classroom and sat next to Jaspa, for some
reason he began to feel weary and tired, he could hardly keep
his eyes from closing, he began to look through his school books
trying to find his induction notes when he came across the piece
of paper that Angel Simeon had slipped in between his books,
he read the words.

REVELATION:14-1

*THEN I LOOKED AND BEHOLD A LAMB STANDING ON MOUNT
ZION AND WITH HIM ONE HUNDRED AND FORTY FOUR THOUSAND
HAVING HIS FATHERS NAME ON THEIR FOREHEAD'S.*

Int: The voice of Mrs Green the lecturer echoed in the classroom
as Stefan read the passage quietly to himself, suddenly
images of unrecognisable places drifted into his mind and
somewhat influenced his thoughts, Stefan slowly but surely
began to tire, Jaspa prompted Stefan to stay awake and pay

attention to the tutor, just then a cool breeze filled the room but none of the windows or vents were open, Stefan suddenly became alert but none of the other students were aware of the change in the atmosphere, almost immediately after Stefan came to his senses the windows shattered with an enormous crash, and in flew Angel Ruen, the consummate son of Angel Ophlyn, with a wing span towering tall, and above the students, as the smell of death was now lingering in the air.

Angel Ruen

And which one of you is the Angelic Son of Hark, speak now and I will hold none of you to ransom if you reveal to me who he is, it is only the son of Hark that I am concerned with, well I'm waiting

Int: The Classroom doors flew wide open and the man with whom Stefan had seen in the doorway reappeared.

Angel Simeon

Hold your tongue Ruen, you have no business or reason to be in this place of study and good practice

Angel Ruen

Simeon, the Guardian and Protector, I might hasten to add, so you being here only confirms my suspicious that the son of Angel Hark is here, associate us if you please

Angel Simeon

Ruen there is a time and there is a place to deal with such matters but you choose with neither tact nor caution, I can easily relieve you from the very breath of the words you now speak, but on this day I will let nature have its way here and spare you the embarrassment

Angel Ruen

To obey the Guardian and Protector and one so heavenly as you, who commands respect, wisdom and experience, over my thirst and desire to know who my rivalry is, but as you are aware he will be in no need of an education

if he is to have any dealings with me, but before I go,
I shall take myself a prize until he comes forth

Ext: Just then Angel Ruen snatches Josephine from the aisles

Angel Simeon
No Ruen! She is innocent to all of this, she has
nothing to do with this Ruen, Nothing!

Angel Ruen
It is done, I am gone

**Ext: Angel Ruen takes off with Josephine Young and flies off
through the shattered window.**

Angel Simeon
Stefan Stiles, come with me quickly

Stefan Stiles
Hey you're the guy from down the hall, what's happening,
what was that thing, where's he taking Josephine, wait a
minute you know my name, how come you know my name?

Angel Simeon
Come with me, there isn't much time, I will
tell you everything and all you need to
know on the way, come we must leave

**Ext: Josephine Young had been grabbed from her desk in the
classroom and pulled through the window, with which Angel
Ruen had made his entrance, Josephine was in a terrible
state of shock, shrieking and screaming as Angel Ruen
headed for the skies, they were by now, in mid-flight and
the shadow of Angel Ruen's wings could be seen over the
earth.**

Josephine Young
Where are you taking me, let me go, please
whatever you are let me go, you're hurting me

Angel Ruen

I am Ruen and you are nothing, do you hear me, nothing, if I
let you go you will surely perish on the ground beneath us

Josephine Young

Then put me on the ground, I'm scared, I'm not use
to heights, you're holding me far too tight, my
arms are hurting, please Ruen, set me down

Ext: Angel Ruen loosened his grip, and Josephine felt herself
falling through the air helplessly, she was afraid, Angel
Ruen quickly swooped down beneath her and once again
caught Josephine in his grip, she was frantic and in a
panicked state of shock.

Angel Ruen

I am simple saving you to protect my interest, you are
merely a pawn and an insurance to get what I truly want,
maybe you know who the Son of Angel Hark is, well do you,
speak now or I will throw you to the earth beneath us

Josephine Young

I don't know what you're talking about, I only met
with the group today, I don't think any one of us
knows anything about anyone in that class, whoever
you're looking for, could be anyone of those boys

Angel Ruen

You lie, tell me what you know or you will die

Josephine Young

Oh God please, why would I lie to you, I'm telling the
truth, honestly I don't even remember any of their names

Angel Ruen

Do you value your life?

Josephine Young

Ok I'm thinking, give me a moment, I think
there's Michael, and Jaspa and he was sitting
next to Benjamin, I can't think of anymore

Angel Ruen

But I saw more than that, tell me who is the other one?

Josephine Young

I'm not sure, I can't think of his name, it might be Steven, or
is it Stefan, yes I think it's' Stefan or something like that

Angel Ruen

Then you shall live to see his death

Ext: Angel Ruen flew high over the built up areas of mountainous
regions, where only wildlife seemed to show any movement,
he had already prepared a dwelling place for himself,
where no one could reach, even if they attempted to climb
up by hand or foot, he set Josephine down in a cavern which
was lit by candles on its' inner walls, as they entered
within, an Earthly smell of Jasmine and Lavender drifted
about the place, which appeared as if it had been in use
for some time, it contained all of which Angel Ruen needed
to survive while waiting out his fateful meeting with the
son of Hark the Herald Angel, Stefan Stiles.

Josephine Young

Are you human, I mean is this really happening, I know Michael
Angelo used to paint and Cherubs, they've got them on the wall
in the Vatican, he was quite famous for his portrayal but they
never looked anything like you, I know, you're a reincarnation
from a previous life aren't you, and you've come back to haunt
me because I did something terribly wrong in my former life

Angel Ruen

So you know very little about Angels and their breed, you
may see them as kind and gentle loving creature, well that's
absurd and purely a myth, that only exist in the minds of men

Josephine Young

So tell me, how can something as hideous as you possess
the power of the immortals and the breath of life?

Angel Ruen

How observant, oh wise child of the earth, so you're not so
naive after all, so tell me how did you come to know this?

Josephine Young

By reading a book, or don't you have any?

Angel Ruen

Damn your books and damn you and your kind, don't you know
that Angels don't just exist in the fantasies and dreams of
the minds of men, although it is unfortunate for you, that
you have indeed ended up with me, I have such little feeling
for you and your inadequate, delicate, weak and puny little
race of people, you and your kind are simply a pastime for
the omnipotent one who with the force of the Herald Angels
brought you into existence, but my uprising will turn back
the tide if not for me then for my beloved father, Ophlyn

Josephine Young

So you're a fallen Angel, a demon, its' no wonder
that you resemble a Black Raven or something

Angel Ruen

A Raven, how very becoming of you to compare me to a bird
of the Harvest, my name is both notoriously known throughout
the whole Angelic Kingdom, if it hadn't been for Hark the
Herald Angel, a champion over these worlds, then my father
Ophlyn, would stand in his place and the earth would be
my sanctuary and playground, and as for you and all the
other mortals you would be only as slaves and captives in
my domain, buy one still remains, Simeon the Guardian and
Protector, he who can reveal the Son of Hark to me, the one I
must defeat and destroy to become ruler over the dominions

Josephine Young

So that's why you smashed through the classroom window,
you knew that Harks' son was there but that other man

stopped you, so he must be Angel Simeon, the one whom
you feared and called, what was it, the Guardian and
Protector, so your just using me as bait to get to
Stefan, in your thirst for power, your evil, pure evil

Angel Ruen

Don't tempt me or I'll have you breathe your last
breath, out of those fragile lungs of yours

Josephine Young

You speak so strongly about negative and destructive things,
as if anyone would allow you to rule over the earth and
destroy everything in its' place, I don't fear you, but I
pity your ugly mind, if you think that by taking my life,
things will change, then you're wrong and its' a ridiculous
notion if you think that your evil ways will win over

Angel Ruen

I sense that you are aware of all things unseen by the
naked eye, how might this be unless you have the gifts
of the earth mothers, this cannot be true, once again
my senses do me well to have captured one such as you,
tell me Josephine, how is it that you came to be, before
I squeeze it out of you inch by inch, I may have need
for you in more ways than I may have anticipated

**Ext: As Angel Ruen questioned Josephine about the nature of her
existence, a cold chill came over him as another presence
appeared, it was Pablo the Immortal, standing at the
entrance of the cavern and Angel Ruen swung around to see
him standing there.**

Pablo the Immortal

You have gone against the omnipotent one by taking
this girl as a prisoner, the forefathers are angry and
displeased with you Ruen, be set right with them and allow
the girl to go freely, there is nothing to be gained by
keeping her here, if you defile her son of Ophlyn and
take of her what she has not consented or agreed upon,
then you will be branded with an iron rod and you will
live out the rest of your days in the soul cages

Angel Ruen

I have laid no hand upon this girl, but she is my
prisoner, because she knows the son of Hark and he
will not come unless he knows that I have her, she is
in no danger, be gone from here Pablo the Immortal

Pablo the Immortal

You have been warned Angel Ruen, the mothers of Tetra
will judge you accordingly to your deeds, be sure and
certain to know that in these days of the last harvest,
it is only the son's of Hark and Ophlyn that should
engage in this battle, there is no need for any more
to be slain, remember that is to be said, I am gone

Ext: **Pablo the Immortal flew into the horizon as Angel Ruen
kept a sharp eye on Josephine huddled up in the corner of
the cavern, Angel Ruen sat across from her and whispered
faintly to himself, as he finished the chant his wings
gradually disappeared back into his body and then he
closed his eyes and went into a deep meditation.**

Ext: **Stefan and Angel Simeon made their way through the streets
of the city, they came to a very large looking house which
appeared to be very eerie and old, as if it were in need
of repair, they were about to enter by a side alley when
Stefan noticed a sign outside on the side wall of the
alley, some kind of billboard which read.**

Ext: **ALL WELCOME TO THE HOUSE OF MADAME MADINIQUE'S** *SPECIALISTS
IN TAROT READINGS, PALMISTRY, A FORTUNE TELLING, CLAIRVOYANT
AND SPIRITUALIST.*

Stefan Stiles

What are we doing here, I thought that we were going to
see a friend of yours, what's her name, Mercidiah?

Angel Simeon

In this city, and in this particular house, is the women
of whom I spoke of, the name which you read on the wall
is only a disguise, you see Madame Madinique is really
Mercidiah, but for her own safety it would be better for all

to keep quiet about it, she is very much loved and respected as an earth mother, and by the spirits of the Tetra

Stefan Stiles
What is an earth mother?

Angel Simeon
When we speak of earth mothers, we think of the tetra, we feel it's' a feminine and maternal presence as an entity or force that resides over us, and we Angels are graced in the tetra's presence, for you to understand this Stefan, you must try to remember ancient stories like that of Venus or Aphrodite, tetra is very much which makes women such as these great forces in the universe, they are made up of the four elements of Earth , Fire, Wind and Sea like the first born of their kind, Eve, the woman who walked the earth, she bares its' fruits and bestows its' gifts upon the earth mothers such as Mercidiah, who is truly a gifted and talented woman with great knowledge of her kind, she is blessed with the tetra, and she has the vision and the foresight, to see into the future and read the minds as well as the hands, she interprets dreams and speaks of premonitions, but be warned Stefan, should any man disrupt or interfere with all that is of the tetra and belonging to an earth mother, his soul is damned to an eternity in the soul cages, nothing can ever return to its' former life if this happens, the spirit can no longer be housed in its' temple

Stefan Stiles
Tetra, Earth Mother, Eve, Aphrodite, what does all this have to do with that thing flapping its' wings and taking off with Josephine?

Angel Simeon
Earth Mothers, are the chosen ones of womankind who can bare the Angel Babies, I too will soon have to consummate my love with Mercidiah, she has already consented to me but my time has been focussed on you, but I tell you Stefan my life spell will soon come to an end and it will be time for my final eclipse, if this should happen before we mate then I shall become an

immortal such as Angel Pablo, I have brought you here for preparation to meet with Angel Ruen, come let us enter

Stefan Stiles
You mean that thing was an Angel, wow
man! This is all too fantastic

Int: Inside Madame Madiniques, Stefan and Angel Simeon make their acquaintances known.

Mercidiah
Its' a pleasure to meet you in person Stefan, Son
of Hark, I have been expecting you to come for
some time, but it would seem that you are a little
disturbed by this event, well there is no reason to be
alarmed, I can assure you, so please take a seat

Stefan Stiles
Hi, I mean Hello Mercidiah, yuh know I find all this
a little hard to believe and I'm just a little bit
uncomfortable by all the action I've seen lately, I
must tell you Mercidiah, where I come from they don't
look upon witchcraft as a promising livelihood

Mercidiah
Witchcraft! I must say that you amuse me Stefan, I didn't
think that a young man of your age would be so ignorant
and afraid as to not be able to distinguish between the
difference, of a prophetess and a woman who supposedly
walks around with a black cat and a bubbling cauldron,
I'm afraid you're out of date which is o.k. although some
of the things I do may be considered the practice of an
occultist nature, but all I really do is simple guide
and help some of the people who need my services

Angel Simeon
Mercidiah, there is little time to be discussing
the finer point of your job, we must tell Stefan
the true nature of all he needs to know

Mercidiah

Listen Stefan, and listen well for the son
of Ophlyn will try to defeat you

Stefan Stiles

And who might that be?

Mercidiah

His name is Ruen, he is very dangerous and a force to
be reckoned with, Angel Ruen possesses the curse of the
Angels of Death, and he will attempt to destroy or defile
the earth if allowed too, but first he must overcome
you, son of Ilark, he will try to kill you and in doing
so nothing will stand in his way, the second harvest
is simply between you and Ruen, and no one else can
interfere, but be warned many lives are depending upon it

Stefan Stiles

What the hell am I involved in here, first I'm told
I have to face the Angel of Death, then I'm told I'm
gonna have to save the world and a girl I hardly
know, so tell me what's the next thing, I suppose I'm
gonna sprout wings and fly around the room, I can't'
believe that I'm even here discussing this with you

Angel Simeon

You seemed troubled Stefan, tell me what is it that
worries such a young man, still in his prime of life?

Stefan Stiles

Its' funny you ask such observant questions, I
mean is it ever present in my facial expressions or
mannerism of something, of course I undoubtedly have
something on my mind, either you two are completely
cracked or I've been abducted by some crazy people

Angel Simeon

Well rest assure Stefan there is nothing to worry
about, based upon my own intuitive nature, I can also
see beyond the obvious, it should only be of concern

to you that what you are experiencing, is a natural
development of what you are about to become

Stefan Stiles
You make it sound as if I were about to mutate
or something, I'm not an alien you know, but
I sure got my doubts about you guys

Angel Simeon
No we are not Aliens, but you may well
soon, become something much more

Stefan Stiles
What do you mean?

Angel Simeon
I mean you may well soon start to experience certain
changes in your physical body, that is not let's say exactly
concerned with adolescence, it is possible for you to
change or as you might say mutate but I would associate
it as more of an ability to metamorphosis from a half
human to a complete Angel and back again if need be

Stefan Stiles
Metamorphosis, mutate, who the hell are you kidding,
I knew it, you people definitely have a problem, I
want nothing more to do with you and your crazy
schemes, if you don't let me walk out of here
peacefully I'm going to have to call the police

Angel Simeon
Allow me to tell you about an Angel I once new, once upon
a time this Angel dreamt he was a caterpillar crawling
about the undergrowth of some bushes, living off the plants
and the flowers and taking refuge in the wildlife, he then
lay down to sleep among the leaves in a tree and, finally
he woke up to find that he was a butterfly, flittering and
fluttering about happy with himself and doing as he pleased,
now the Angel who had dreamt this dream, suddenly realised
he was in fact like this caterpillar but the fact that he
was uncertain of, is that we're he an Angel dreaming that

he were a caterpillar that had become the butterfly, or was
he a butterfly that had dreamt that he was an Angel, the
Angel in this story was in fact your father Stefan, Hark,
the Herald Angel, and he told me this story many moons ago

Stefan Stiles
You mean my father was a caterpillar?

Angel Simeon
No! don't' be so stupid and fickle boy, your father is and
was an Angel, and a very good one at that, what I am trying
to outline to you is that a caterpillar becomes a cocoon
and then an adult, and as an adult it is transformed into
a butterfly, the difference between the us, and the Angel
Babies and human babies is that we too experience a period
of change and go from having no wings to having wings, it
is just a question of time before these changes occur

Stefan Stiles
Next you're going to tell me that you're an Angel but
you took your wings off, to look less conspicuous

Angel Simeon
Your nearly right, but not quite on the mark, all we have
to do is simply will for our wings to appear to disappear
and it is done, although initially the first stages are
more extreme, you see although our wings mutate out
of our backs, I must warn you for your sake it will be
your first heavenly Angelic experience and you will feel
a considerable amount of pain, almost unbearable

Stefan Stiles
So I'm going to sprout wings and fly, you must
think I was born yesterday, whatever your taking
jack! They should sell it by the kilo

Angel Simeon
Ok have it your way Stefan, you may mock me, but soon
you will understand by the power of the knowing

Int: At this point Stefan started perspiring and sweating per furiously, as if he were infected by some sort of feverish tremendous heat, he was becoming hotter and hotter, until he could stand the heat no more, Stefan started ripping at his shirt while Mercidiah and Angel Simeon stood back and looked on as the knowing began, Stefan could hardly keep his balance and was becoming more and more confused and disorientated.

Stefan Stiles
What's happening, I feel strange?

Mercidiah
It is the knowing, it has begun, It is the first
signs of Angel rebirth into maturity

Int: The sound of Stefan's voice began to change from a deep tone to a very high pitch as if it were the voice of a baby trying to communicate for the first time, he then fell to the ground, face down and started arching his back as if he were in fits, then began the convulsions as he tried to gasp for air, and then slowly in a half naked state, his wings began to break through the spinal cord and for the first time signs of brilliant white feather appeared on his back, growing faster and longer by the second, Angel Simeon placed his hands on Stefan's head and removed the Seal which had been placed there when Stefan was a child, it was the Seal of Hark and with it being removed the knowing began.

Stefan became the knower, millions of thoughts and images of the past and present flashed and raced through Stefan's mind, flashbacks that seemed to be evident as if Stefan had himself lived through them, time and time again, the First world war and then the Second world war, the Famines and plagues that have wiped away races and races of people, the knowing was a reminder of the first harvest, but a sound which became louder and louder and seemed somewhat familiar to Stefan, it was a fanfare of horns which resounded in the heavens and in Stefan's mind, reminding him and reassuring him once more of what he was and who he was, the reason and the purpose of his being, the calling into Angelhood, and there he stood tall and noble, a tower of strength and beauty with a wing span of twelve feet or more.

Angel Simeon

What you have just experienced was and is the legacy of fallen Angels, the accursed reign of Angel Ophlyn and his kind, In this World, nation fought against nation and famine and disease brought the Earth to its' knees, your father Hark, fought this foe who ruled over these dominion's, it was the first harvest in which many were plagued because they had turned their backs on the kingdom and the heavens, but it was not known to them that it was to be brought down with a vengeance for the renewal of the Earth and her inhabitant's, many people were slain, and as Hark the Herald Angel offered Angel Ophlyn to submit to the will of peace, he yielded not, and so they fought and struggled until a successor would stand, and on that day your father took from Angel Ophlyn, his breath of life, but what we did not know then but found out soon later, was that Angel Ophlyn had impregnated an Earth Mother before his fall, he was to have a son and his name is Angel Ruen, it is he who is seeking you out for revenge over his father's death, it is written in the heavens but it is yet to happen on this day of the Earth and yet it is also the second harvest and it is also time for you to face the future Stefan

Mercidiah

Stefan the future has presented itself, but your position is as yet, unclear, from the telling of the signs and the energy forces I am getting a reading from the girl, i feel that she has the seventh sense and the insight, it may well be, that she is blessed with the spirit of the tetra, but Stefan you must understand that no mortal can kill an Angel, he can only be overcome by one of his own kind, and when this happens, the spiritual body of an Angel leaves the physical form and the human form is left once the act has been done, this also happens once an Angel has consummated his love with an Earth Mother, these are metaphysical changes that takes place in all of you, unless you become an Eternal Immortal. Angel Ruen will try to carry out his

father's will and judgement upon you, as you must carry out
yours, you must defeat Angel Ruen before the evil reign of
history repeats itself, You must also take in you the bowl
of indignation which is offered to you, the horns in the
heavens will be sounded and Hark the Herald Angel will sing

Stefan Stiles

Then tell me, what is the way of he who came before me?

Angel Simeon

The way of he who came before you is demonstrated not without
the need for the justification of all things, but is also
pursued in the advancement for peace throughout the world,
for reasons being that all which is good must be gathered
up in the last harvest, Angel Stefan, Son of Hark arise and
hear me when I say to you that your bringing about this
judgement should not be seen as the be all and end all in
the purpose of the Angelhood in which you are called to
serve, nor should you give in to any guilt of the testament
of your will, but instead you should use your powers wisely,
for the contempt of Angel Ruen has brought about a demise
and near destruction upon the Earth and our heavenly angelic
ancestry, I now turn over to you this bowl of judgement,
which you must sip and then pour out over the earth just
before you sip the morning dew when you take flight, it
alone holds within it, the bitter truth of innocent blood,
which has been slain since the legacy of fallen Angels
began, redeem them this day Angel Stefan, redeem them

Stefan Stiles

If it is only damnation for the damned, then how
can I execute good judgement over the innocent?

Angel Simeon

The innocent are of no concern to you Stefan, the
way of the World as Mercidiah puts it, is itself
already written by the will of the Omnipotent

Stefan Stiles

Then I question this will on the merit of
my being and what is required of me

29

Angel Simeon

But Stefan, you would not be here if it were not for the will
of the Omnipotent, and its' presence in you, if you choose
to question what you are then you must ask yourself what am
I, what is an Angel and in by doing so you become the lesser
of the two, and indeed you would have fallen, if a human
were to question what he is, whether man on mammal he too
will become the lesser of the two and find that he is only an
animal in the jungle, on this instruction Angel Stefan, I now
say go and do your will for it cannot be denied the truth

**Ext: The windows flew open and by a quick shove of Angel Simeon's
right hand, he then simply jumped out, but as he leapt he
whispered a short chant and his wings unfolded and streamed
forth from out of his back and he flew upwards, as he did
this, he extended his arms to Angel Stefan to follow suit,
And so it was that Angel Stefan leapt through the window
and took to flight, they were both now high above the city,
the people below seemed to be of little significance and
importance as they gazed down upon them.**

Angel Simeon

Now that you are in touch with the skies, I will teach you
how to use the elements of the air and the wind beneath
your wings, this will be to your advantage in battle, you
must fly like the Eagle and soar down upon you prey from a
great height, you must be able to control you movements in
mid-air and flutter your wings like the delicate humming
bird as she feeds upon the nectar, you must then be able
to pluck your prey form the currents of the wind like a
kingfisher that dives into the waters below, come we will
try some manoeuvres of defence and attack, after all Angel
Ruen is no fool in the skills of these flying acrobatics,
but one can accomplish much here in the skies and with your
strength and ability he may well find you a worthy adversary

Stefan Stiles

I feel so free and alive, its' so wonderful up here Simeon,
its' great, I feel as though I could fly forever and the skies
upon the horizon, it goes on forever and ever, its' magnificent
up here, how come you never told me all this before?

Angel Simeon

Is it only now that you choose to believe what I have been
trying to tell you all along, yes up here its' another world,
it is freedom unparallel, and that is at the heart of all
you have to do, we have little time in preparing you for your
confrontation with Angel Ruen, so look around you Stefan,
and look into your heart and remember what this means to
you and those who came before you, and those of us who may
come to know the skies, you have the knowledge to deal with
such a foe as Angel Ruen, but I tell you now Stefan the
breath in which we breathe is a whisper, a chant, it is the
word that informs and transforms our senses, it also tells
us much more about what is near and what is far, whether
there is danger present and whether the dew is ready to be
sipped, the dew of which I speak, is at this point in the
skies, and is the dew which lines the clouds, we must sip of
it the pureness and the richness before it touches the Earth
below, An Angel takes several breaths before he sips this
dew and at this point he becomes vulnerable for he must open
his mouth and it is then that your mouth must meet his, and
suck the ethereal breath of life that he holds within him,
but be warned for the taking of the ethereal breath of life
will empower you immortality that may make you unconscious
or disorientated for a little while, so be sure to take every
breath from his living body in order to be certain of victory

Stefan Stiles

You mean to tell me that I'm gonna have to kiss his light's
out, that's disgusting, surely there must be another way

Angel Simeon

There is no other way Stefan, but know this, he will also
try to do the same to you, such an opponent as Angel Ophlyn
and your father Angel Hark fought for days in an attempt
to take the ethereal breath of life from one another, but
enough talk of the past, it is now the future that is at
stake here, and now it is time for you to pass the judgement
by sipping and then pouring out the bowl which you possess

Stefan Stiles

I'm afraid, I'm afraid to do it

Angel Simeon

Fret not thyself Stefan, and do your will

Ext: Angel Stefan slowly brought the bowl to his lips and tasted the wrath of fallen Angels, he then tipped the bowl with both hands and watched its' contents evaporate into the air stream suddenly there was silence, as there was now flashes of lighting above the clouds and the skies had confirmed it, the thunder began to roar, and on the distant horizon the skies began to grow darker until eventually, everything was filled a blackened and dusty mist, suddenly time stood still and so to were Angel and Stefan as they hovered in the air, the judgement had been made and nothing could prevent it from happening, Stefan looked all about him and remained indifferent, but he thought why did things have to come about this way, Angel Simeon also remained beside him but said nothing, time stood motionless until Stefan could stand the silence no more.

Stefan Stiles

What happens now?

Angel Simeon

Now we wait for judgment to pass

Stefan Stiles

What has happened to the time, there's
nothing, nothing at all?

Angel Simeon

That's' because there is nothing

Stefan Stiles

Then when will we see the light of day?

Angel Simeon

Alas, the light of day

Ext: At that very moment, the very second that Stefan spoke the whole world lit up again, as if Stefan had commanded it,

the sun came shining through the clouds as it had never
shone before, all thing were truly bright and beautiful
and Stefan was amazed and bewildered then he had contained
the power of the word in speech to change that which
almost brought him to fear his own heart.

Angel Simeon
It is done, he will come

Stefan Stiles
You mean Angel Ruen?

Angel Simeon
Yes!

Ext: After Angel Simeon and Stefan took to flight, Angel Ruen had
already woken up from his deep meditative sleep and flown
from his cavern high in search of Stefan. Josephine Young
was still left huddled up, cold, alone and defenceless
not knowing what fate would befall her, Angel Ruen had
become aware of the scent of Angel Simeon and Stefan in
the skies, Angel Ruen was ready and charged to fulfil his
pledge and avenge his father's death and to take rule over
the dominions in his father's name.

Angel Simeon
He is near, I feel the cold chill of death in my senses and
his scent is in the air, you must prepare to face him

Stefan Stiles
And you Simeon, what will you do while
I'm making love to the opposition

Angel Simeon
I cannot interfere in any of this, I am old and
weary and very tired of battle, you are young and
strong and of the new revelation, I will simply be a
watcher and an observer of all that takes place

Stefan Stiles

And if he wins, If I am beaten, what then?

Angel Simeon

Have you forgotten your father, if it is not an understatement on my part then I must say that I bid you not to take this lightly, but you must believe me when I tell that when Hark the Herald Angel sings, anything is possible

Stefan Stiles

I don't hear any singing

Angel Simeon

You will

Ext: Angel Stefan, after heeding the words of Angel Simeon flew off high into the skies where the clouds separated the heavens from earth, he then sipped of the dew that lined the clouds and felt his entire body shiver with life which somehow seem to charge through him into his blood and bone, then Angel Ruen appeared flying in from the distant horizon, coming closer and closer, until he too reached Angel Stefan.

Stefan Stiles

It is not my will to take another's life especially your, so why do I feel that you want to take mine, surely we can work this thing out?

Angel Ruen

I see that you have the fear that only man possesses, so tell me son of Hark what does it mean to be a dream maker who has a broken dream and dreamed no more?

Stefan Stiles

What does that mean, what is this, a guessing game?

Angel Ruen

What does it mean son of Hark or have you never dreamed?

Stefan Stiles

Of course I dream

Angel Ruen

Then pray tell me the answer

Stefan Stiles

If I'm right then it simply means that innocence and
sincerity have somehow been denied promise and truth

Angel Ruen

And tell me Angel Stefan, when will become of the dream maker
will he forever sleep or will he awaken, with his dreams of
promise and truth intact, with its' sincerity and promise?

Stefan Stiles

Dreams, truth, promise and sincerity, that's a
bit of a riddle but I guess, but the dream maker
can only awaken, when the dream comes true

Angel Ruen

My dream is this Angel Stefan, I will destroy you and you
shall die, now you can die slowly or you can die quickly, I
shall break you in two so that your dream will die with you,
and the rest of your soul shall become a living nightmare,
eternally damned in the soul cages, that is if you ever find
a way out of it, it shall be to you an unbearable nightmare
just as to me the loss of my father was also unbearable

Stefan Stiles

Hey Ruen now it's' my turn to talk, tell me,
have you kissed any girls recently?

Angel Ruen

What do you mean?

Stefan Stiles

I mean the girl you took, well you see she's
a friend of mine, and I was wondering if you
infected her with the same disease you got?

Angel Ruen

You toy with words and mock me, for that I will hear no
more of you, not even a sigh or a whisper, shall fall from
your mouth, when I take from you the breath of life

Ext: Angel Ruen grabbed Stefan's throat and suddenly began to
squeeze it harder and harder, they both began to struggle
as Stefan fought back for control, by now they were both
hurtling and falling in a downward spiral toward earth,
both of their wings flapping violently to try and gain
stability.

Angel Ruen threw Stefan down to the ground below and was now
flying downward to finish him off, Stefan quickly reacted and
soon stood to his feet and once again he was airborne, he headed
directly towards a cloudy point in the skies and once again
sipped on the dew, he then turned to see Angel Ruen rapidly
approaching, they both flew at one another until they collided,
Angel Ruen swung Stefan around and then held him from behind
into a headlock, he then tried to twist Stefan's head so as to
break his neck in order to weaken him and take the breath of
life.

Stefan now being in an awkward position began flapping his
wings strongly and dived with Angel Ruen still on his back,
towards the ground below, then in a mighty forward roll half
way between the ground and in mid-air Stefan made himself flip
into a forward roll, Angel Ruen was thrown off Stefan's back
so fiercely that Angel Ruen crashed into an abandoned building
below, it was now time for Angel Ruen to stand to his feet but
as he did Stefan came rapidly flying at him from such a height
and with such great force that he managed to kick Angel Ruen
in the chest, Angel Ruen went rolling and tumbling across the
rubble and wasteland of the deserted the building, gasping for
breath Angel Ruen lay there.

Stefan stood over him and looked down upon him, for a moment
he remembered catching Josephine's eye in the classroom and
then the sunlight flashing in eyes, Angel Ruen still remained on
the ground, neither of them moved, no one uttered a word, Stefan
looked around for Angel Simeon who he could barely see, but he
could just make out a small figure of him on the distant horizon,
once again Stefan took to the skies, but this time he flew in

the direct path of the blinding sunlight and then suddenly he vanished in its' stream of sun rays.

Angel Ruen couldn't believe it he had been spared and stood up and looked around towards the heavens, by now Stefan had reached Angel Simeon and told him to observe no longer but that he should look and seek out the whereabouts of Josephine Young, Angel Simeon obeyed and left his watching place.

Angel Ruen was once more airborne but he could not see Stefan anywhere in the skies as the sunlight shone to brightly, As Angel Ruen flew across its' path a hand came out or nowhere so swiftly that it caught Angel Ruen by surprise, Stefan grabbed him by the throat and in sudden state of shock he opened his mouth and as he did Stefan held his head with both hands dragging Angel Ruen higher and higher into the skies, Angel Ruen continued to struggle in an attempt to break free but he was losing concentration on keeping his mouth closed, and so as he panicked to loosen Stefan s grip.

Stefan was pulling Angel Ruen's head closer and closer to his, and just before Stefan put his mouth up against Angel Ruen's, at this point Angel Ruen tried to sip the dew but it was too late, Stefan squeezed at Angel Ruen's throat and in a deadly kiss, took from him the ethereal breath of life, it was done.

Stefan Stiles

I call upon heaven and earth to witness against you this day that you will soon perish from the land which you choose to possess, you will no longer spend your days in the heavens as your soul will become condemned in the soul cages, I gave you the opportunity to obey me, for I am merciful but you chose to ignore me in judgement of the wrath of the fallen Angels, I now forgive the past but ask now concerning the days ahead that the son's of Angels become redeemed from one end of the earth to the other, and unless we forget this day I shall be a witness for any peoples speaking out of the midst of the fire that no other Angel had sought to undo this before me, if this is my inheritance then let it be known, that my will is done

Ext: Pablo the Immortal appears in the sky.

Pablo the Immortal

Hark the Herald Angel, your son Stefan the conqueror, Stefan son of Hark, you have returned to us somewhat broken in spirit but alive and well, it will be a great reunion this day in the heavens and I Pablo the Immortal will commence your bidding

Stefan Stiles

Come Pablo the Immortal, we must fly to the abode of Mercidiah and seek out Josephine and Angel Simeon

Mercidiah

Stefan you've returned, but where is Simeon?

Stefan Stiles

I sent him to find the girl, Josephine Young, don't worry he will be here shortly

Mercidiah

And what of Angel Ruen, where is he, what has happened, did the two of you engage in battle?

Stefan Stiles

It is done, my will is done, and so too is my father's will, Angel Ruen, remains defeated by my hand, if there could have been another way I would have taken it, but it is done, my will is done

Mercidiah

Your conscious bothers you, you always seemed deeply concerned with the truth of things, as too was your father, he also regretted his actions

Angel Simeon

Who regretted?

Mercidiah

Your back and you have brought the girl with you, is she well?

Angel Simeon

She is well, and still very much pure in heart

Stefan Stiles

Hey Josephine, its' good to see you again, are you Ok?

Josephine Young

I'm fine, but look at you Stefan, I can't believe it,
you're an Angel, its' almost too good to be true

Angel Simeon

It is written that an Angel who descends to consummate
his love with an earth mother, that his time spell
will end, in order for a successor to live on

Mercidiah

But Simeon, he is the son of Angel Hark,
and the harvest has now passed

Stefan Stiles

Then what you are trying to say, is that I must take Josephine
as my chosen earth mother, to commit the act of finality

Josephine Young

No Stefan, what Angel Simeon is trying to say, is that he
is ready to and willing to commit himself to Mercidiah,
but can I add that I am willing to be yours, if you accept
me as your earthly bride and breathe into me the breath
of life, then I will be yours throughout eternity

Stefan Stiles

How do you know this?

Josephine Young

Simeon told me all about it, and you, and Angel Ruen, and the
second harvest, and all that is ripe must be gathered up

Angel Simeon

It is my time now Stefan, but it is wise for you to
choose to take Josephine as your earthly bride in the
future, as she has all the virtues of the mothers of Tetra
inside, my time spell is already elapsing into eternal
immortality, I must fulfil my commitment to Mercidiah

Stefan Stiles

Very well then, I will give to Josephine what no other mortal woman of her kind possesses, the breath of life

Int: Josephine now begun to close here eyes and open her mouth as Angel Stefan now the conqueror, put his lips up against her mouth, she trembled and shuddered with such frailty, as his body towered over her, Stefan then blew his breath into her mouth and released the very essence of life itself into her being, she begun to sigh and moan, as a feeling of regeneration overcame her.

Stefan closed his eyes and began kissing Josephine with a grace of softness and of the love that he intended for her, and it was done, the earth mother Josephine Young was born, just then as Stefan began to open his eyes, he was now no longer standing in the humble lodgings of Mercidiah's home, but was somehow transported through his actions and by the power of the love of heaven, to the dwelling place of his father, Hark the Herald Angel.

Hark the Herald Angel

Pablo the Immortal summoned you here at my bidding

Stefan Stiles

How be it that I should stand here before thee and see thee and speak with thee my father, have you not transcended the abode of the mortal realm, while my mother, Selah is only a silent memory, or have I awakened to find myself in the afterlife for my actions?

Hark the Herald Angel

By the sound of the horns in the heavens, all of those who sleep and dream of the morrow are soon awakened from sleep by the promise of eternity, it is by my will that I once again reunite with you, I mean after all Angel Stefan, all that is well, ends well, now listen to the music, isn't that beautiful, how sweet the sound, and now you know by what faith and promise does the Herald Angel come, you and I are both hidden from each other amongst the Immortals, and yet in an eternity although we may die a thousand times and so be it, we shall still by the will of the knowing, live on, do you doubt this, my son?

Stefan Stiles

I do not doubt what I am father, but it comes as some surprise to me that we are reunited, I understand now that it is by the will of the knowing that you stand here before me and I before you, although in time you have slept for an eternity, until Pablo the Immortal who never sleeps wakes you, and by your bidding the sound of the horns in the heavens are sounded and your will is done, but father allow me once more to return from whence I came, the place that I call home, for my returning here has reassured me of who and what I am, even though it has been for a short time, I do recall my childhood and I remember being held and loved by the grace of my family who taught me how to be a man, strong and kind. Sometimes the memory fades into war and deceit, but then there is also the dream, this dream of the Angel Babies, whose world is filled with a kind of magic and wonder, for which many, even those of us with the simplest of lives have made their sacrifices for, but you and I, if we are immortal then there is no need for a succession, this is only this beginning, so allow me once more to sleep father, for I am aware that you watch over me always, and I extend my heart and hand to you always as your son and between the heavens and the earth, I will once more dream of you

Hark the Herald Angel
Stefan awake, awake Stefan

Int: In one moment Harks voice become Jaspa's voice.

Jaspa Alal
Stefan awake, awake Stefan

Stefan Stiles
Hey what's up man, quit nudging me

Jaspa Alal

You keep falling asleep, if you don't pay
attention you're going to miss out on what Mrs
Green is saying about social curriculum

Int: Stefan looked around to see if the window had been shattered
but it was just the same as when he had caught Josephine's
eye. The sunlight streamed into the classroom just as
before that moment, when everything seemed to change.

Stefan Stiles

Social curriculum, what are you talking about,
what's happened, where's Josephine?

Jaspa Alal

She's sitting right over there, are you sure
your o.k. You keep falling asleep, you must be
dreaming about Josephine or something

Stefan Stiles

Yeah, something like that

Int: Now Stefan Stiles was only sixteen when he defeated his
foe and archrival Angel Ruen. Several years had passed and
Stefan was about to graduate from University. Now no one
could have been prepared for what was taking place in the
underworld, nor could they have prevented the course of
events that would inevitably lead us to the soul cages and
the coming forth of Papiosa.

ANGEL BABIES
THE SOUL CAGES

Ext: It is' night time and the stars are shining brightly over a shanty town somewhere in a remote village in Africa. Over previous years the land has been subject to famine and by now only yields very little crop for food to eat, and these shanty town dwellers are to weary to go in search of greener pastures in order to aid their survival or indeed prolong their imminent suffering and inevitable death.

Ext: There are only but a few watering holes to drink and wash in and yet still only fewer plants and trees that have edible fruit fit to eat for human consumption but it is within this scattered community of broken souls that Papiosa who is looked upon as a down and out ill-fated man, is often seen talking to himself in a half dazed and confused state by his onlookers, who often chooses to isolate themselves away from him in their reproach of him.

Int: During the night after foraging around for food and in the undergrowth, Papiosa returns to his dilapidated remains of a shack and lays down upon his makeshift bed made of old clothing and worn bed sheets, gazing out of a hole in the roof looking up at the stars casting their light over his shadowy face now dimly lit by the moonlight. Just then the silence is disturbed by a voice quietly calling out.

The voice of Angelo

Papiosa, Come forth

Papiosa

Who is it, who's there?

Int: Feeling somewhat frightened and fearful, his eyes widen as he withdraws further beneath the sheets, once again the voice is heard.

The voice of Angelo

Papiosa come forth

Papiosa

Who is it, what do you want?

The voice of Angelo

I want to show you something

Papiosa

Show me what, I do not know you, and I have already seen what there is to see?

The voice of Angelo

No! Papiosa, that is not true, you have not seen what you wanted to see

Papiosa

But how come, how do you know me, how can you know what I have or have not seen?

The voice ofAngelo

Because I want to show you something

Ext: Suddenly in a flash Papiosa is running as fast as his feet can carry him, desperately and frantically as if being pursued, and then once again in flash he is back where he was, lying down upon his bed looking up at the stars

The voice of Angelo
Why are you running Papiosa?

Int: Papiosa feels confused.

Papiosa
Running…

The voice of Angelo
You were running away from something, why were you running?

Ext: Papiosa is silent

The voice of Angelo
Do you remember when you were born Papiosa,
do you remember the dream?

Papiosa
What dream, I have no recollection of any dream

The voice of Angelo
Every night you have the same dream Papiosa,
don't you remember, the one in which you are
running, come forth and I will show you.

Ext: Once again Papiosa is running for his life, breathing heavily and sweating from his brow with the sounds of people in the background as if he is being pursued by an angry mob, and then once again he is lying down in his dwelling place looking up at the stars. And upon reflection he becomes agitated.

Papiosa
you are obeah?

The Voice of Angelo
No Papiosa I am not

Papiosa
You are Juju?

The Voice of Angelo

No Papiosa I am not

The voice of Angelo

What I am does not matter Papiosa but if you must know one thing about me then remember this, that I have come with the waters of time inasmuch that I am eternally coming and going forth like the seasons, as to what is to become before me, then know that I am also like the tears of heaven giving way to an endless stream that gives way to the oceans and when the rainfall ceases in its' down pouring, I am like the deluge and the raging waters that recede if only to rise again in the vain hope that I may gather myself together, if only to calm the stormy seas that somehow seem to gather and form like endless clouds, that journey along set adrift upon the edge of memories year after year, I am also like the morning dew before the sun has time to set sail upon its endless journey from east to west, until time itself has remembered to forget who I am, or why I have come, or where I am going, but tell me Papiosa do you remember when you were born

Papiosa

When I was born, but I cannot even remember one day to the next, how can I remember when I was born, it was so long ago, one day I was with my Mother, we were happy, she was happy, everybody was happy, life was good, we use to hunt for fish and make clothes, and sing songs, yes I can begin to remember a thing or two, why do you ask me this?

The voice of Angelo

I ask you this because, you asked me

Papiosa

I did not ask you anything.

The voice of Angelo

But you did Papiosa, don't you remember, just before your Mother passed away, when the famine came, do you remember, you said you wanted to live forever, you said you wanted everlasting life, **Papiosa**
I don't remember, when did I say this?

The voice of Angelo

When you were a child Papiosa, when you were a boy

Papiosa

But I do not remember, but anyway I have said
many things as a boy that I don't remember

The. voice of Angelo

It is easy to forget a childhood dream Papiosa, it
is even harder to forget hardship and suffering,
come forth Papiosa I want to show you something

Ext: And once again Papiosa is running aimlessly and endlessly
through the bush land, in a frantic panic trying to escape
something or someone, and then in a flash, he wakes up
sitting in his bed in confusion and bewilderment, as if he
had just had a bad dream.

Ext: The next day Papiosa is fishing in a nearby stream as the
other settlers are wearily nearby doing the same if all
but nothing else. Papiosa is feeling somewhat disturbed by
the night before, now believing it to be a bad dream and
nothing more, and then once again as night falls and he
returns to his slumber, and he hears the voice again.

The voice of Angelo

Papiosa, come forth

Int: Suddenly Papiosa sits up in shock as if disturbed by a
ghost.

Papiosa

Who are you, what do you want?

The voice of Angelo

I want to show you something, come
forth so that I may show you

Int: This time Papiosa, stands to his feet and walks out of his
shack into the opening but see's no one.

Papiosa

Where are you?

Ext: As everything falls silent, a light appears in the distance, which Papiosa, walks towards as a sign, as Papiosa walks towards the light he hears the voice.

The voice of Angelo

I want to show you something that you cannot and
will not forget, unless you fall asleep

Papiosa

Why me, why have you chosen to show me and tell me this?

The voice of Angelo

Because shortly I want you to understand,
what is to become of you?

Papiosa

But I am only a simple man, what am I to do once
you have revealed your knowledge to me?

The voice of Angelo

You will understand, what to say and do, once you have
grasped the understanding of my revelation to you

Ext: And so as Papiosa continued to walk, seemingly into the wilderness talking to himself in pursuit of a light, that never seemed to standstill or become within reach of, as the voice began to instruct and influence his every move and thought.

The voice of Angelo

There are several realms and several depths to the
heights of heaven, and the earthly plains below, I
cannot explain all of them to you as it would take you
several lifetimes in earthly years to expand upon the
embodiment of this knowledge to you, but each realm
is open to its own interpretation once you arrive

Papiosa

Arrive! Arrive where, where are we going?

The voice of Angelo

Firstly we are going to the tetra valley where you are
dreaming, where the stars can be seen more clearly,
from this point you can begin your ascent from there

Papiosa

But where is this place, where do I sleep?

The voice of Angelo

They themselves will reveal to you the abode of the Angels,
this place is your first step upon the ladder to eternal life

Papiosa

But what if I do not want to live forever?

The voice of Angelo

Then you shall die forever

Papiosa

But how come, surely a man can only die once in his lifetime?

The voice of Angelo

If you believe this, then look at the past again

Ext: Once again Papiosa is running through the wild forestry,
this time, we can clearly see that he is being pursued by an
angry mob of settlers who are desperate if not determined
to kill him, because they are under the illusion that he
brought misfortune to their village, and so frantically
he is fighting his way through the forest and bush land
until he comes to clearing which is a swamp area of mud
and oil, but before Papiosa can think to avoid the sodden
quick sand land he is already knee deep into the mud,
slowly beginning to sink and drown until eventually he is
swallowed up whole and remains to be seen no more, and as
the last few air pockets bubble up to the surface all is
still, and it is at this precise moment he wakes up in his

dwelling place gasping for air and for breath, occasionally looking up at the stars, shouting out loud.

Papiosa

What do you want?

The voice of Angelo

I want to show you something

Papiosa

But I died

The voice of Angelo

Yes you did upon this plain, that's how you were meant to die

Papiosa

Then how is it I am here?

The voice of Angelo

You are here because you called out to me in your dream

Papiosa

But I don't remember

The voice of Angelo

Do you remember the famine Papiosa, when the rains finally came, after the famine, after your mother died

Papiosa

Yes but why do you keep asking me that?

The voice of Angelo

Because it is easier to forget a childhood dream and even much harder to forget hardship and suffering

Ext: Just then Papiosa is back in the wilderness walking toward the light

Papiosa

How much longer will it take?

The voice of Angelo

It will not take much longer you must rest here until tomorrow

Ext: Just then Papiosa sets down to rest and almost instantly falls to sleep through tiredness and exhaustion, and once again he begins to dream the same dream having reached the clearing and is now sinking into the swamp until he is swallowed up whole, and at this precise moment the embodiment of an Angel covered in blackened oil comes shooting out of the swamp like a winged creature brought to life out of the murky depths concealing a bow, dripping with the silky slimy oil that covered it from head to toe, and then takes aim and shoots an arrow into the heavens, saving the fearful Papiosa who now awaits to see what he would have to remember as heaven begins unfolding its secrets from the depths so deep, with realm after realm flashing like constructs and constituent parts of a whole in the form of a hierarchical projection giving insight and meaning to every part of his minds interpretation, imagination and understanding

Ext: Papiosa was now locked into its celestial body absorbed into a transcendental state of shock and awareness through mental bewilderment, beauty, awe and wonder, instantly recognising and realising the Empyrean realm and the abode of the Angels and then again in a flash is instantly running through the forestry, and then seemingly seeing his own death and as if transported through a phenomenon of several worlds colliding both interacting and interchanging at will reconfiguring and rearranging instantaneously until it vanishes to be seen no more, except him beside himself in his own mortality laying down beneath the stars.

Papiosa

What is this place?

The voice of Angelo

The abode of the Angels

Papiosa

Why did you bring me here?

The voice of Angelo
Because I wanted to show you something

Papiosa
Am I to be grateful?

The voice of Angelo
Only if you choose to be

Papiosa
I don't know if I am grateful or afraid

The voice of Angelo
You!

The voice of Angelo
Fear is the beginning of wisdom

Papiosa
Who am I?

The voice of Angelo
You are Papiosa

Papiosa
Who are you?

The voice of Angelo
You know who I am, I am the message bearer

Papiosa
But why me, why now, what message?

The voice of Angelo
Because it is time

Papiosa
Time for what?

The voice of Angelo
It is time for me to go

Papiosa
Go where, from where did you come?

The voice of Angelo
From where thou dwellest

Papiosa
Empyrean?

The voice of Angelo
You remember?

Papiosa
Yes, yes I remember

The voice of Angelo
Why you are running?

Papiosa
Because of time

The voice of Angelo
There is no time, time is immortal

Papiosa
Yes, time is immortal and time is also running out for Papiosa

The voice of Angelo
Then where will you go?

Papiosa
I shall begin my descent from here and then
I shall go to the furthest realms

The voice of Angelo
Remember Papiosa, remember what you have
seen, shall not be seen again

Papiosa

How can I forget, unless I sleep?

Int: And instantly Papiosa is transformed, Meanwhile a faint shadow dwells in-between the worlds in a place of purgatory known only as the Soul Cages, it is Angel Ophlyn the father of Angel Ruen.

Angel Ophlyn

Yin men shen, yin men shen, I chant thee the incantation of yin men shen, dark guardians of the door, I ask thee, grant me safe passage from the depths of these cages, yin men shen, I chant thee the incantation to the keys that free the soul, free me from the domain of the one called Papiosa, **Papiosa** The guardians of the door cannot heed your call Ophlyn, the key to the soul cages are within my keep now and mine alone

Angel Ophlyn

You think you are the first to possess the key, but before you there was I you cannot hold me here forever, I still speak with the tongue of Angels

Papiosa

But you are without configuration, there is nothing here to house the embodiment of your soul, your only hope was your son, Angel Ruen but he was defeated by Angel Stefan, son of Hark, now you are both lost to me, this passage cannot be broken or overcome

Angel Ophlyn

Yin men shen, yin men shen, I chant thee the incantation of yin men shen, guardians of the door, free me from this animatism of the cavea, break the doctrine of the otachuk cavea! Jiva! Liberate Ophlyn from this Jiva cavea!

Papiosa

When will you learn Angel Ophlyn, there is no redemption here for you, not until you fulfil the doctrines of Samsara, which only permits that none may influence the transmigration of the soul until he has completely

fulfilled the judgements of the first harvest and has become
reconciled in full, only then all deeds of action of a
former existence are vanquished, and so in doing, you must
forgive and forget in order for you to become a new being

Angel Ophlyn

Ophlyn never forgets, I shall never submit, I chant
thee the incantation of yin men shen and the dark
guardians of the door they will heed me

Papiosa

Once I was pursued and persecuted for the mockery of a foolish
idea that what I believed was true to me even in the eyes and
the minds of those that did not accept or choose that what I
was subject to, soon found me excommunicated and pushed away
from the very people and the things that were most precious
and dear to me, I mean the very idea that a soul can be
caged or at least cast out and contained in the belly of a
fish strikes me with profoundity, but faced with the idea that
a body of flesh, blood and bone can become decayed overtime
and give way to the very plants and insects that are fed and
nurtured upon its' destruction is not so implausible, and
now I am taken even further away still into other worlds,
which in all its' beauty is still beset upon by the most
profound, if not absurd idea of all, that whomsoever is
blessed let no one curse and whomsoever is cursed cannot be
cured unless he fulfil his redemption in a cage fit for a soul.

Angel Ophlyn

Ophlyn cannot be, nor will not be, caged like a bird

Papiosa

Oh! But one can Ophlyn, just as it said that one day
war shall breakout in the heavens, sending shockwaves
through the heart of creation and as for all the fallen
Angels like yourself, shall be expelled from the pillars
of the firmament forever more, and you shall become no
more than slaves of servitude to mankind, and who knows
maybe one day, even you shall evolve into the species
known as man a befitting judgement don't you think?

Angel Ophlyn

A man! A man is no more than a wretched creature upon the face of the Earth, how can a man live amongst the stars as I do, you speak as if you had known these things all along

Papiosa

Ophlyn you were given over to me simply because you have fallen from grace and forgotten the virtues that were bestowed upon you so long ago, I myself am a being made anew and I now know my role and my duty and my calling, and so therefore I must fulfil my obligation as for my former life before this awakening tis' no more but a page in my history never to be spoken off again and off little use and meaning, but now, now I am restored to serve as an integral member of this ethereal world both above and beneath us.

Angel Ophlyn

But you are nothing compared to Ophlyn, nothing except a gate keeper waiting in the wings for souls, only to be found sleeping until their unexpected and oblivious awakening.

Papiosa

Yes! But had there not been anyone here to watch over these simplest of life forms, how would they have slept in their comfort free from the fear that every soul should or could be plundered, and had not even you so desired to be free from your destiny who knows we may never have even met, I mean Ophlyn, Angel Ophlyn the one who once flew with Hark the Herald Angel, can you believe it, my how the mighty have fallen, and who is to say that your actions are not pre determined, even in this execution.

Angel Ophlyn

Papiosa, you are a fool to think that I can become as nothing, I am more than An Angel of the highest order.

Papiosa

But you seek vengeance, is that not an Earthly property Angel Ophlyn I Seek justice!

Papiosa

Then I am your judgement

Angel Ophlyn

No!

Papiosa

Yes! You see, you must consider it as an act
of your retribution and determinate vengeance,
it is a foolish ambition to believe otherwise,
accept your fate and face the consequences.

Angel Ophlyn

You threaten me with words you know very little about

Papiosa

Then so be it, in seeking passage into a world of temporary
existence where all things must eventually expire, then if the
guardians of the door open to you, I shall not prevent you
from crossing over to your death, as much as I know it may be
impossible for you to feel jealousy or indeed put piety before
pride, but does that not mean you can easily become defied by
disappointment with so little time to turn back the clock.

Angel Ophlyn

What do you mean?

Papiosa

I'm afraid it's time.

Angel Ophlyn

Time for what?

Papiosa

Time for me to go

Angel Ophlyn

Go Where?

Papiosa

Well in case you were not aware time has already transcended
and yet there is so little time to do so many important
things, but I must leave you and depart company inasmuch
that I have enjoyed what little time you have left.

Angel Ophlyn

You have brought me here and sought to deceive
me with this trickery and false illusion, and
for that reason I shall smite you.

Papiosa

Without configuration, tis' easy to forget

Angel Ophlyn

You are a conjurer and a thieving magician, I shall
find my way through this maze of confusion.

Papiosa

No one can escape the cages my friend, no one, for there is
nowhere to go and nought else to do, you are truly alone.

**Ext: As Angel Ophlyn took to flight, the skies above had become
a blur of clouds, drifting and reforming into a landscape
of nothingness.**

**Int: Meanwhile the Earth Mother Kali Ma begins to experience a
mild premonition in the presence of Mecidiah.**

Mercidiah

Kali what is it, you seemed troubled

Kali Ma

I'm not sure, something seems to call to
me, don't you sense it, its' strange

Mercidiah

I haven't picked up on anything since you went into
a sort of daydream, but then again I know that you

have a deeper connection with the underworld than I
do, it could be anything or nothing, couldn't it?

Kali Ma

No Mercidiah, it is much more, much, much more, as earth
mothers we must pay close attention to all disruptions, even
the faintest callings or whisper's are important to our psyche

Mercidiah

So what are you saying Kali?

Kali Ma

I am saying that the abode of the dead are waking
and something very terrible resounds within my soul,
something is very, very wrong, I can feel it, its'
as if evil it trying to make its' presence known

Mercidiah

Come sister, hold my hand and let me share the
medium with you, we can meditate together

Kali Ma / Mercidiah

Who is the whisperer of these ancient names,
what is your purpose, and why are you here?

Angel Ophlyn

Otahchuk Cavea! Free Me! Yin Men Shen! Jiva
Cages, Free me! Free me from the soul cages

Kali Ma

It whispers the names of Men Shen Mercidiah
The guardians of the door

Kali Ma

Yes but that is an ancient incantation, its' originality
is a dialect from the eastern scriptures

Mercidiah

So who is the summoner of such ancient spirits?

Kali Ma

I don't know, but no doubts it is something or someone
who is very knowledgeable on the old ways, I can feel
it bursting with anger and rage, as if …as if its'…

Mercidiah

As if what, Kali Ma?

Kali Ma

As if it were alive

Mercidiah

Impossible!

Kali Ma

No Mercidiah it is not, perhaps in the place of the soul
cages or the Otachuk Cavea, the summoner may be trapped
there, it may even be that it is dead but it is without
rest and such spirits can only be the bearer of bad
tidings, it somehow has a will of compelling destruction,
and that is why it is calling out, it is unfulfilled
and I also believe that it is seeking possession

Mercidiah

So what must be done to re channel it,
if it poses such a threat?

Kali Ma

Even now we have empowered it by reaching out to answer
its' questions, we must inform all of the earth mothers
to resist opening up to any temptation to understand this
anima, and hopefully it will resolve itself in time

Mercidiah

And if it doesn't stop, what if it keeps beckoning

Kali Ma

Then there will be no peace for it or us unless we
mediate and control our powers to deal with such

unlikely entities, we must channel our energy to re-
direct the anima back through the cages

**Int: Meanwhile Stefan Stiles is at university being awarded for
a graduate exam.**

Mr Jacob Day

Well Mr Stiles, it seems that you have achieved an above
average score once again on your grade paper, I must also
commend you on your presentation, which I might add will
be more than suitable for you to succeed in any future
pathways if you intend to carry your studies further

Stefan Stiles

Thank you Mr Day, I don't know what to say

Mr Jacob Day

Say nothing my boy, it's been a pleasure to have been a tutor
to such a radiant and grade A student as yourself, no doubt
you and the expectant Mrs Stiles will have something to
celebrate on this particular occasion apart from the pregnancy

Stefan Stiles

Yeah, I guess we will

Mr Jacob Day

So will you and your wife be taking any
excursions, or breaks this summer, Stefan?

Stefan Stiles

Yeah, its' funny that you asked, we plan to relax on
the coast, Josephine's got some friends down there, who
knows, maybe I'll take up fishing or just go for some
relaxing walks, along the coastal lines, who knows?

Mr Jacob Day

Very good, very good, well you shall be receiving notification
of your pass mark and graduation certificate by post, officially
of course, but we know a pass when we see one, don't we"

Stefan Stiles

Thanks again, Mr Day

Mr Jacob Day

No trouble, no trouble at all, and by the way Stefan,
you can call me Jacob, its' quite acceptable

Stefan Stiles

Oh Ok, Mr Day, I mean Jacob, I guess that's it, thanks and
goodbye, thanks for everything, its' been a great year

Mr Jacob Day

Goodbye Stefan

**Ext: Stefan was feeling quite excited about the exams and on
top of the world about his graduation pass mark from
University, he couldn't wait to get home to tell Josephine
the good news.**

Josephine Young

So tell me, how was it, good, bad, medium, average,
well c'mon, the frustrations killing me

Stefan Stiles

You won't' believe it Jose' just before Principal
Day calls me into his study to comment and
congratulate me on my thesis and presentation…

Josephine Young

So you passed then

Stefan Stiles

Yeah, I passed but I was as nervous as hell

Josephine Young

What do you mean nervous, I thought religion and
history was your thing, I bet you walked it

Stefan Stiles

Well yes, No! Well I tried to cover a broad philosophy of religion from a historical point of view, yuh know while being topical on such points as voodoo or black magic and spiritism

Josephine Young

Go on, it sounds interesting

Stefan Stiles

Well I kind of went into early medicine men and ancient rituals which then opens up to the first enlightenment of breaking the rules of tradition and convention you know towards the reformation, which then leads us to self discovery and the exploration of our ancestors or indigenous practices, which initially forms our concepts of spirituality, this then went onto the application of new approaches, which extends into achieving a balanced mind by developing and adapting old and used methods with new concepts and approaches by reason of definition of course which lead me to new man his ability to advance beyond our own natural world into what I term, 'supernatural phenomena

Josephine Young

Supernatural Phenomena

Stefan Stiles

Yeah you know, the ability to understand the higher self and, good karma, and the final enlightenment, which I actually believe encompasses the way to completeness of the body and mind by way of meditation of course, whereas the awakening is one of pure realisation, which allows us to recognise that in our own personal experiences, we are fundamentally becoming a universal race of people which I believe puts God at the root of creation

Josephine Young

Sounds like complete crap to me

Stefan Stiles

Oh Josey, don't be like that

Josephine Young

Only kidding, you mean you really got through all that and everyone really understood what you were talking about

Stefan Stiles

Yeah well I may have got a few heads thinking, but I'd rather talk sensible crap with you, than fill your head with nonsense

Josephine Young

Yeah right, well you said it Stef

Int: Back in the soul cages Angel Ophlyn is still resisting his judgement, and his influence is affecting the Earth Mothers.

Angel Ophlyn

Free me

Josephine Young

What did you say Stef?

Stefan Stiles

Nothing, Why?

Josephine Young

Oh, Ok

Stefan Stiles

Why what was it?

Josephine Young

I'm not sure, I don't know

Stefan Stiles

What is it, is it the baby?

Josephine Young

I don't think so

Stefan Stiles

Then what's wrong?

Angel Ophlyn

Yin men shen! Otahchuk Cavea, Free me!
Free me from this cage where this Jiva Cavea holds me

Josephine Young

There it is again

Stefan Stiles

What?

Josephine Young

I thought I heard something, didn't you hear it?

Stefan Stiles

No! I didn't hear a thing but there is
one thing I forgot to mention...

Josephine Young

...Mention, what did you say?

Stefan Stiles

I said there's one thing I forgot to mention

Josephine Young

Mention, yes, it sounded like mention or
men shen, I'm not quite sure

Stefan Stiles

Yeah mention, yuh know about our little break, yuh know
out of the city, hey Jose' are you even listening?

Josephine Young

Yeah I'm listening

Stefan Stiles

Are you Ok?

Josephine Young

No! Yes! I mean I don't know, I think I
just had my first premonition

Stefan Stiles

Yeah Ok, what was it?

Josephine Young

It was strange, you were trying to find me but you
were somehow trapped in this place, but I could see
you fighting for my life, you were struggling to break
free, but it was helpless and I could do nothing to
help you, I saw you die Stefan, I saw you die right in
front of my eyes and I could do nothing about it, it
was so real, I can't believe it, It seemed so real

Stefan Stiles

Hey Josie, its' alright, don't worry, its' just the
pregnancy taking so long, its' got you worried

Josephine Young

I don't know, maybe your right, I never felt like
this before, but I don't want to lose you, not now,
not ever, you know you're my God of love, don't you,
my Eros, my Cupid, I love you, I really do

Stefan Stiles

And you're my Goddess of love, my Aphrodite, my Venus and
you'll never lose me, not now, not ever, so don't' worry

Josephine Young

Your right, God knows what got into me, it was only
a word, I'm sure it was nothing, its' silly really,
c'mon you get the car ready, were going on this
holiday and nothing's going to spoil it, Ok

**Int: As Josephine and Stefan are currently underway on their
holiday, driving along the highway, Mercidiah and Kali Ma
are having difficulty in contacting them.**

Mercidiah

I have managed to get in touch with all our sisters
except for Josephine and Stefan, but I am certain that
they were planning to go down to the coast for a break

Kali Ma

We must take no chances, they must be
contacted and informed right away

Angel Ophlyn

…Free me…

Josephine Young

What did you say?

Stefan Stiles

Nothing, why?

Josephine Young

Oh!

Stefan Stiles

What is it, is it the baby?

Josephine Young

Stefan, something's wrong, I can feel it

Stefan Stiles

Well tell me, what do you want me to do?

**Int: Suddenly in the car Josephine becomes completely possessed,
as Angel Ophlyn manages to transgress the soul cages.**

Josephine Young / Angel Ophlyn

I want you to free me from the soul cages

Stefan Stiles

Josephine! What's got into you?

Josephine Young

No! Stefan look out were gonna crash

Ext: **The car swerves off the road and into some trees and Josephine is knocked unconscious, Stefan manages to gain some control but is also badly bruised by the accident. But taking effect in the mind of Josephine Stiles, Angel Ophlyn has somehow managed to influence her and is attempting to manipulate her will, so that he can control her soul from within.**

Angel Ophlyn

Josephine, free me

Josephine Young

Who are you, where am I?

Angel Ophlyn

Free me, I can help you

Josephine Young

What is this place, you spoke my name,
how do you know my name?

Angel Ophlyn

I am Ophlyn, I can help you

Josephine Young

Ophlyn, Ophlyn tell me where I am, what are you doing here?

Angel Ophlyn

I am a victim like you, in this place, it is known only
as the cages of the soul, it is the dwelling place of
Papiosa, we are all trapped here, but you are free,
you can help us, you have been sent here to free us

Josephine Young

If I help you will you help me to get back?

Angel Ophlyn

I will, yes I will help you, now free me
before the immortals descend upon us

Josephine Young

So how do I free you, I don't know what to do?

Angel Ophlyn

You must command me to come into you, the
guardians of the door will do the rest

Josephine Young

But I have a child inside me

Angel Ophlyn

Fear not Josephine, I will not harm the child,
such an infant is protected by Angels

Josephine Young

But how can I trust you, how do I know if you are not fallen

Angel Ophlyn

Fallen, Angel Ophlyn fallen, it is not so, ask
yourself this Josephine, how be it that I know you
by name, when it is only the cages that divide us

Josephine Young

But how can I free you if I don't know the
commands, that the guardians have granted you

Angel Ophlyn

Just ask the guardians at will

**Ext: As Josephine speaks the incantation she is tricked into
summonsing Angel Ophlyn into her world.**

Josephine Young

Yin Men Shen, Guardians of the door, I command thee to
grant Ophlyn safe passage through the cages into me…

Ext: Just then Ophlyn takes possession.

Angel Ophlyn
YES! Yes Ophlyn Lives, I must make use of you
before the guardians descend upon me

Ext: Josephine becomes unconscious, as Angel Ophlyn take possession.

Josephine Young
No!

Angel Ophlyn
No doubt this will be a day of reckoning
for Angel Hark and his counsel

Ext: At the roadside Stefan is attempting to revive Josephine.

Stefan Stiles
Josephine! Wake up, c'mon Josie, wake up, oh
no, what have I done, Jose c'mon, can you
hear me, Jose… somebody please…help us

Ext: Just then Angel Simeon appears.

Angel Simeon
Do not despair Stefan

Stefan Stiles
Simeon, please help us, I think she's dead

Angel Simeon
Place your hand beneath her bosom

Stefan Stiles
She's warm

Angel Simeon
Then her heart still beats

Stefan Stiles
Then what's wrong with her?

Angel Simeon
I fear the worst has happened, she is
inhabited possibly possessed

Stefan Stiles
By who, by what, tell me Simeon?

Angel Simeon
I fear it is none other than Ophlyn

Stefan Stiles
The father of Ruen, but Ophlyn was slain by Hark, he's dead

Angel Simeon
Somehow Angel Ophlyn had passed through the door of the soul
cages, if she is possessed then Ophlyn resides in her soul...
...Speak Ophlyn, I command thee to release this girl

Josephine Young / Angel Ophlyn
You dare to challenge me after you took my son
from me, this girl will become my host until I find
Hark and carry out my retribution on his head

Stefan Stiles
No! This can't be, how can this happen, this can't be Simeon?

Angel Simeon
You must take her body to a place of safety

Stefan Stiles
I need to see my father

Angel Simeon
You cannot see your father until he has
summoned you, I will carry out your will

Stefan Stiles

But time hangs in the balance Simeon, Josephine could die and she's pregnant, what about the baby, where is my father?

Angel Simeon

Take her to a hospital, I will inform Mercidiah what has happened, it is only Angel Hark who has the power to decide the fate of this transgression, you must wait until he has requested your presence beside him, now go while there is still time

Int: Somewhere in the Empyrean.

Pablo the Immortal

The trumpeters have sounded the arrival of Angel Simeon

Hark the Herald Angel

But I have requested no union at this hour

Pablo the Immortal

Then I fear it may be something of dire importance, as he is the guardian of your son

Hark the Herald Angel

You fear, or you know, which is it?

Pablo the Immortal

It is…

Angel Simeon

I must inform you Angel Hark that Ophlyn has gone beyond the passage of the soul and entered in Josephine Young

Hark the Herald Angel

How be it?

Angel Simeon

He tricked her by way of the guardians of the door

Hark the Herald Angel

Is she dead?

Angel Simeon

No, but she is in limbo and critically ill

Hark the Herald Angel

Then I must awaken my son before all else is lost

Angel Simeon

I have sent for Mercidiah and her sister
Kali Ma to attend to her needs

Hark the Herald Angel

Then it may be possible to stop the transmigration
of her soul into the underworld

Pablo the Immortal

No doubt Papiosa will try to gain advantage of the
situation, he is both conning and deceptive, it
may even be that he allowed this to happen

Hark the Herald Angel

Then I shall seek counsel with him, come we fly

**Int: As Angel Hark and Pablo the Immortal and Angel Simeon make
their way to the abode of Papiosa, Mercidiah and Kali Ma
have all gathered at the hospital to meet Stefan.**

Mercidiah

Stefan, we came as soon as we got word, how is she?

Stefan Stiles

I'm not sure, she's been admitted to an intensive
care unit, the doctors say that she's' suffering from
a concussion after the crash, she's also delirious
and falling in and out of consciousness

Mercidiah

We must see her, its' imperative to her well
being, if she is indeed possessed by the spirit of
Ophlyn then it could kill her at any moment

Stefan Stiles

But what can we do?

Mercidiah

I've brought my sister along to help us, she has
a gift and a craft of the underworld she also
knows about the transmigration of the soul

Kali Ma

Tell me who is the Doctor in charge here?

Stefan Stiles

I'm not sure, I think his name is Bestillus

Kali Ma

I'll ask a nurse.., excuse me could you tell me
which practitioner is in charge of Josephine Young,
she was recently admitted into intensive care?

Nurse

Yes its' Dr Azif Bestillus, he's in charge of the operation

Stefan Stiles

Operation! What operation?

Nurse

I'm afraid you'll have to wait until he completes
his assessment, as you know Mr Stiles, your Wife's'
condition is critical and I'm not at liberty to
comment on any procedures at this stage

Kali Ma

How is she?

Nurse

I'm afraid she's still comatose, but I guarantee you
that we are taking every care and precaution to reduce
any damage to the brain and ensure the safety of the
unborn child, Dr Bestillus will be with you in a moment,
he will inform you of all that you need to know

Kali Ma

Can we see her?

Nurse

The Doctor will give you notice of that, I'm afraid
that's all I can say at this time, I'm sorry

Mercidiah

What do you think?

Kali Ma

Well I fear the worst, the more time
elapses, the more danger she is in

Stefan Stiles

So what will happen Kali Ma?

Kali Ma

All I can tell you Stefan is that as earth mothers we are
both knowledgeable and spiritually informed of things which
are I might say are not of this world, we are vessels which
house the spirit of mother nature herself, and therefore
their motives become our desire, my body is in subjection
to their instruction and so therefore I must mediate and
choose wisely the path that I may take, all this must
be thoroughly examined and thought through before any
decision can be taken, this is how we learn and grow, it
is the sanctity and the principle teaching of all earth
mothers, I must attempt to counteract the incantation

Stefan Stiles

So how does this affect Josephine?

Kali Ma

Josephine is of a lesser maturity and therefore she is
inexperienced with these matters, Ophlyn will try and take
control but even the host spirit needs to feed on the soul,
he will also attempt to dictate her activities but this can
only happen once she is awake, while she sleeps the real
battle is within, if she becomes possessed by the inhabitant
of the spirit, then it could defile her, I must try and break
the spell and prevent this from happening, but you must also
play a part Stefan and face Papiosa or Ophlyn in the cages

Stefan Stiles

I must see my father only he can help me...
where are they, what's keeping them?

Mercidiah

Be calm Stefan, this worry will solve none of this

Stefan Stiles

But she's dying...

Kali Ma

Look the Doctor is here, we must be calm for Josephine's sake

Dr Azif Bestillus

Mr Stiles?

Stefan Stiles

Yes?

Dr Azif Bestillus

Well I can tell you that Josephine is stable for
now but she has sustained some injuries to her
head which may cause some slight brain damage
unless she wakes up out of the coma very soon

Stefan Stiles

So the longer she's unconscious, the worst
it could be for her, is that right?

Dr Azif Bestillus

Yes

Kali Ma

And what about the pregnancy, is the child in any danger?

Dr Azif Bestillus

Well, we've been monitoring the child's heartbeat and
we may have to induce the pregnancy, if she remains
critical, fortunately the chid is unharmed at this
time which is very lucky but I will let you know my
decision once this probationary period has passed

Mercidiah

And how long is that?

Dr Azif Bestillus

A few hours, no more

Stefan Stiles

Can we see her?

Dr Azif Bestillus

Yes you can, but only for a short while

Kali Ma

Thank you Doctor

**Ext: Stefan enters the hospital room by stands by Josephine's
bedside.**

Stefan Stiles

Josephine can you hear me, Josey

Mercidiah

She is weak, Ophlyn dominates her soul

Kali Ma

Yes its' true, she is consumed with a
sickness, we must attend to her

Stefan Stiles

But what can be done Mercidiah, what will turn her around?

Kali Ma

Talk to her Stefan, maybe the sound of your
voice will comfort her, it may help

Stefan Stiles

Josephine can you hear me, Jose listen, I love you, how can
I tell you how much you mean to me, I miss you, I miss you
so much, please babe, you're my Goddess of love, remember, my
Aphrodite, my Venus, Josephine please don't die, I love you,
I really do, if I could do anything to turn back the hands of
time, believe me Jose, I would, Jose please, come back to me

Mercidiah

She stirs, but she sleeps among the dead

Kali Ma

If she is utterly consumed then Papiosa will take
her, I must attempt to pray for her deliverance

Stefan Stiles

Who is Papiosa?

Mercidiah

Tell him

Kali Ma

Papiosa was a man seeking divine and infinite knowledge of
the abode of the Angels, and many times he studied the
ancient scriptures' of the Seraphim's and the Cherubs to
try and learn the mystery of the Heavens and how Angels
manifested and revealed themselves in human form, in
Papiosa's attempts to research the relationship between us
and them, he soon realised that through cross conception,

that the earth mothers and Angels conceived of divine
life forms, which Papiosa soon realised surpassed the
expectation of mortal life forms and that these souls
possessed a certain spirit in the anima which is also why
the passage of the anima or soul was placed in the eye

Mercidiah

That is why the eyes are the window to the soul

Stefan Stiles

I don't understand, what does this have to do with Josephine?

Kali Ma

Well just before his death, it is believed that Papiosa saw
the face of four Angels descending upon him in the Tetra
valley, this is what we call 'Tetra Anima', but what Papiosa
did not realise, was that in his attempts to learn the
mystorics and the abode of the Angels he had neglected himself
to the point of selflessness, Papiosa became obsessed with his
search for wisdom and understanding, and if he could indeed
live a better life in the hereafter, was all that concerned
him, but after long deliberation and searching in the Tetra
valley, no matter how much Papiosa meditated on the principle
of the four faces, his own soul was departing, by now Papiosa
had started to lose consciousness through the lack of food and
sleep and in the last moments of his life force ebbing away
from him, Papiosa saw a face looking right at him, it was his
own face amidst the vast space of nothing around him except
the valley, it was frightening and at this point Papiosa died
and as it is told, he became the keeper of the soul cages

Stefan Stiles

So if Papiosa is the keeper of the soul cages,
why can't we just get him to free her soul?

Kali Ma

Because the four Angels who first carried Papiosa to the
abode of Heaven were, Hark, Simeon, Pablo and Ophlyn

Stefan Stiles

Ophlyn! Why, What, I don't understand, Ophlyn?

Mercidiah

Stefan, before you were born Ophlyn and Hark were friends
but when the earth mother Selah offered herself to Hark
as a consummate bride, it caused a rift between Hark and
Ophlyn, as Ophlyn desired your mother, the one we call
Selah, who so happened to be in love with Hark, this angered
and displeased Ophlyn which is one of many reasons why
Ophlyn lost favour and fell from grace, the rest you know

Stefan Stiles

So what does this mean, that I the son of Hark slayed
Ruen because of my father's disputes with Ophlyn

Mercidiah

No Stefan, because he would have slain you

Kali Ma

What you must do when you are summoned by Hark
is to travel the path of Papiosa and negotiate
for the safe return of Josephine's soul

**Int: At this point in time Hark the Herald Angel, Pablo the
Immortal and Angel Simeon had reached the dwelling place
of Papiosa.**

Hark the Herald Angel

Papiosa! Reveal yourself

Papiosa

I am here, but tell me Hark, what is the nature of your visit?

Hark the Herald Angel

You know very well why we are here

Pablo the Immortal

The soul of the one known as Josephine concerns us

Papiosa

Souls may come and souls may go, each one is the same to
me and yet different from every other, I have desired to
possess the souls of Kings and Queens and that of vagabonds
and slaves and yet there is not a day that has not passed me
by that I have not sought to possess the soul of a guardian
Angel, they are to me a demon alike, only at the opposite
end of the spectrum, but then again I am Papiosa the keeper
of the soul cages and now I am tempted to possess the soul
of one so innocent and so young, and yet she is barely an
Earth mother who holds virtues as precious as the salt of the
Earth itself and I see you are here to inquire of her passage
through this domain, but her whereabouts remain a mystery

Hark the Herald Angel

Don't tempt me Papiosa, where is she?

Papiosa

No doubt you understand it was necessary to allow
Ophlyn a key to the guardians of the door and so
unfortunately, Josephine just happened to be that
very door that misfortune would open, as for Ophlyn,
it was an opportunity that fate could not resist

Pablo the Immortal

And you allowed this to happen?

Papiosa

Let's just say that I didn't stop it from happening, you see
because of Angel Ophlyn's unrelenting desire to seek revenge
was no longer amusing to me and I thought I would see as to
what lengths he would be prepared to go through to fulfil his
ambitions, I mean after all two souls are better than one

Pablo the Immortal

You fool, you've meddle in matters for too deep
for you to fathom, it is both a damning and
irreconcilable action which must be undone

Papiosa

Undo, but I have done nothing

Hark the Herald Angel

By doing nothing, you have allowed the evil of Angel Ophlyn
to manifest, you must return him to the cages at once

Papiosa

And what say you Hark, if I do not?

Hark the Herald Angel

They'll be no plea bargaining today, if you don't return
Angel Ophlyn beyond this realm and into the next, then
surely you bring down the wrath of Hark upon you head

Papiosa

But Hark has no influence here, unless he barqains with
the one very thing that I wish to possess, as you are
aware I am very meticulous and particular where it
concerns the souls of guardian Angels and now I hold
in my possession, something of a prize to which I might
hasten to add can easily be exchanged for something more
valuable and worthy of my domain, don't' you agree Hark?

Hark the Herald Angel

Hold your tongue Papiosa, before it is
removed and used as a paper sealer

Papiosa

Remove it if you dare, I have no use for it
anyway, as you know it would suit me well to
see you take action and strike against me

Hark the Herald Angel

You fool, don't you see that this is not about me,
why don't you stop this madness and do my bidding

Papiosa

Because Ophlyn has his uses, while he is free I know that
you cannot rest nor find any peace, and this pleases me

Pablo the Immortal

Listen Papiosa and listen well, for was it not us who
first woke you when you were in the Tetra valley, were
you not saved by the grace of guardian Angels, when you
sought to sacrifice your very own soul for the knowledge
and wisdom of Angels, which you now possess and this is
how you show your gratitude, what has become of you?

Papiosa

Because Pablo, I have learned things you cannot imagine,
I have seen things that you cannot believe and now I know
there is much more to everything than I have ever known
before and I am not easily persuaded to part with what I have
obtained, especially now that I know that there is just a
little more to gain, no matter the eloquence of the tongue or
the prudence of your nature, I say only this to you, if you
have something of value with which you wish to part, then I
may consider in returning Angel Ophlyn to the soul cages

Hark the Herald Angel

But there is nothing, there is nothing with which I possess
that can satisfy you desire, surely you can see that Papiosa,
if Gabriel were here he would tell you the same thing

Papiosa

But it is not Gabriel that I seek, nor is it Raphael,
nor is it Uriel, it is of course you Hark

Hark the Herald Angel

That's ridiculous, it's an impossible request

Papiosa

Not impossible

Pablo the Immortal

You ask for too much Papiosa

Papiosa

If Josephine's soul is such a precious prize then I can only
suggest that another soul should be wagered to take her place,

that is if you are willing to make the sacrifice, I mean
after all it is only a just and noble gesture that you should
compensate me for my time, so tell me Pablo who shall it be?

Hark the Herald Angel
Enough! Where is the soul of Josephine, Now!?

Papiosa
She is where Ophlyn speaks from within her, the real
question for you to answer is, where is Ophlyn?

Hark the Herald Angel
Well if I must seek to challenge Ophlyn once
again to stop this madness, then I shall

Papiosa
I find this to be a challenge of interest Angel Hark, as
Angel Ophlyn has manage to manifest his influence between
two worlds, you may need to realise this transition, or
you could fail in your intentions to find the girl

Pablo the Immortal
Hark, you must summon Stefan, he may be of importance
to our choice of action, if Stefan remains asleep
then we will not be sure if it is really Josephine
that will be saved, you must wake him

Ext: Hark the Herald Angel begins to awake his son Stefan.

Hark the Herald Angel
Stefan …Stefan awaken thee the sleeper in me, awaken
thee the dreamer in me, awaken thee reality

Stefan Stiles / Hark the Herald Angel
Awaken the conversation, the time the place we met,
the scene now set and if understood for a moment,
all that is revealed remains timeless and asleep,
peace becomes its' keeper, the dreamer, awaken

Stefan Stiles

Thank you father, its' been a long time but
am I fully conscious of you now?

Hark the Herald Angel

Stefan, sometimes we are awake without knowing but still it
would be better to answer a question with another question
because that way we both have something to think about,
so yes my son, we are conscious now, it seems it has been
too long a time and yet it is as thou time has never
really parted, but tell me Stefan what of Josephine?

Stefan Stiles

She is tormented while she sleeps, and I fear for the
safety of our child, she knows nothing of the hours
that pass us by as if she is held by a spell

Hark the Herald Angel

Tell me Stefan, who speaks from out of her
mouth, is it Ophlyn or is it herself?

Stefan Stiles

At first it was her own voice, but then it became
as if another had taken hold of her

Hark the Herald Angel

I must be certain of Ophlyn's position that is why I ask
you, if I am to take the ethereal breath of life from her
body then there must be no mistake in whose soul is saved

Stefan Stiles

The possession took place in my car, she spoke
in an old dialect, I did not understand it,
but I am sure that Ophlyn resides in her

Hark the Herald Angel

What say you of this Simeon?

Angel Simeon
I say that if the fourth passage of the cages has been broken, then Ophlyn can only truly exist somewhere in this realm and that Josephine is in no real danger while Kali Ma and Mercidiah watch over her

Pablo the Immortal
Papiosa tell us where is the ghost of Angel Ophlyn?

Papiosa
The ghost of Angel Ophlyn only seeks to wreak havoc upon the heads of those it has been imprisoned by, you must look death in the eyes to search out the truth

Pablo the Immortal
Death has no eyes

Papiosa
Exactly!

Hark the Herald Angel
Then Ophlyn is still in the cages

Stefan Stiles
No father wait, I'm not sure

Hark the Herald Angel
Does her heartbeat?

Stefan Stiles
Well yes

Hark the Herald Angel
Then let me face Ophlyn alone, I summons thee Ophlyn from within the place that you hide, stop the charade and reveal yourself

Josephine Young / Angel Ophlyn
Stefan help me, Please

Int: **An apparition of Josephine appeared in front of Stefan, which led Stefan to believe that it was really Josephine standing in front of him, but in truth it was the Ghost of Ophlyn who had by now manage to manipulate and re- channel Josephine's energy into his own.**

Stefan Stiles

Wait father, its' Josephine

Angel Simeon

What trickery is this?

Stefan Stiles

I tell you it's' her, let me go to her

Hark the Herald Angel

No Stefan! Wait!

Stefan Stiles

Josephine look at me, are you Ok, Josey say something?

Josephine Young / Angel Ophlyn

Stefan my cupid, kiss me

Pablo the Immortal

No! Stefan, it could be this kiss of death

Hark the Herald Angel

Stefan No!

Int: **But It was too late, Stefan had placed his lips up against what he believed to be was Josephine.**

Angel Ophlyn

You are too late Hark, now I have my revenge, one life for another, now you can watch your son die before your eyes

Stefan Stiles

Father, Hark, help me

Pablo the Immortal

Its' too late, he draws his last breath

Hark the Herald Angel

No!

Papiosa

There is another way Hark

Hark the Herald Angel

Why should I listen to you, when you are the cause of all this

Papiosa

Did I not offer you an alternative, but you
thought you were better than I Hark

Hark the Herald Angel

Return my son to me at once

Papiosa

And by doing so, do you offer your soul in exchange Hark?

Hark the Herald Angel

I agree

Pablo the Immortal

No Hark, let me

Hark the Herald Angel

But Pablo, do you know what this means?

Pablo the Immortal

I have walked the eternity of time, from one end
of the heavens to the other, and as an immortal
it is only natural that my spirit should come to
rest in the cages, I tire of adventure Hark

Hark the Herald Angel

But I cannot let you do this Pablo

Pablo the Immortal

No Hark please, allow me

Int: Pablo the Immortal kisses Stefan and allows Ophlyn Soul to come into himself.

Hark the Herald Angel

But never again will we exchange adoration with
one another, your soul will become forever mortal
and born again if ever you desire in a distant
lifetime from now, is that what you wish

Pablo the Immortal

It is… if it means that Stefan can live out the rest of
his life with his beloved, then I consider it to be an
honour to have had you as a trusted friend and Herald

Hark the Herald Angel

Pablo, never again will we reminisce the dream of ages

Pablo the Immortal

This dream for now is over Hark, but as for
you Stefan come now, kiss me and allow the
remains of Ophlyn;s soul to reside in me

Angel Simeon

Quick, revive him

Pablo the Immortal

Come Stefan and drawn breath from me

Int: Stefan is revived by the breath of Pablo the Immortal and then his father Hark had also breathed a little life back into him but unfortunately for Pablo the Immortal in helping Stefan by taking on the ghost of Angel Ophlyn is now fated to end with Papiosa in the Cages.

Angel Simeon

He is weak, his spirit is broken

Hark the Herald Angel

Stefan If you stay here you will become an eternal immortal such as Pablo, but if I return you to world then never again will I be able to see as you stand before me today and you shall live out the rest of your days as men do, so now you must choose, which is it to be

Stefan Stiles

Father I can only choose to live out the rest of my days in the world as men do, Josephine is everything to me and all that I can convey in my moment of truth is my love for her

Hark the Herald Angel

Then the only connection between you and I Stefan will be your son, for when he is born he will know nothing of this hour but he will come to embrace the ways of Angels and those s who have gone before him, and as it is written in the Heavens this day what you and Pablo have done to save the soul of the earth mother Josephine Young, will once again become a part of a dream from which you will not wake, not until you have lived out the rest of your lives, but in this parting I promise you we will wake again

Angel Simeon

And who is to take guardianship of the unborn child?

Hark the Herald Angel

Yes I am willing, no doubt the influence that Angel Ophlyn may have had on Josephine, may have caused a lasting and effect therefore I decree and proclaim that the Son of Stefan shall be called by the name Angelo, and let it be known, that this day in the heavens, the whisperer of secrets, shall be a sentient laid so low, that he shall walk where other Angels fear to tread, as a wanderer without wings until he is reconciled once again, back within the Empyrean realm

Stefan Stiles

Thank you father, but what of Pablo?

Hark the Herald Angel
Papiosa, how say you?

Papiosa
So now says Papiosa, that Pablo the Immortal one has made
supplication to give up and render his soul to me and
I am fed and satisfied, and my only stipulation is that
he must submit however willingly, to also walk beside
me wherever these illusions may be cast before me..
...and how say you Pablo?

Pablo the Immortal
Yes I am willing

Papiosa
And you do this simply because you so wish it to be
that the son of Hark may once again walk among men?

Pablo the Immortal
Yes

Papiosa
I am impressed by you loyalty to the Herald, and I must
say it is a noble sacrifice that you make, but let me
ask you this, what kind of Angel are you that I should
accept you in place of Hark, or indeed his son Stefan

Pablo the Immortal
Because I am faultless

Papiosa
Never before have I seen, nor has there been in the
history of the keeper of the soul cages one as would
commit such a selfless act as you, you are indeed perfect

Pablo the Immortal
And there will never be another such as I Papiosa

Papiosa

True Pablo, very true, but then pray tell me Pablo before you accompany me to your destiny, how be it that one such as you has acquired the faith of such deference without a display of modesty, I mean after all surely it becomes you?

Pablo the Immortal

Well Papiosa before you take me under, I must tell you that it would take me three times over to explain to you the history of the world, for one such as you, to truly understand what I have seen, from my conception and birth right through to this very day, there is none that can fathom or surpass the very revelation of this awakening, even the dreamers who sleep only to realise that in waking, they are indeed still dreaming, only then will you realise that time and time again that I have measured the defeats and victories of mankind the world over, but still somehow they manage to survive if only to carry on in the sacred name of love, it is in this understanding that I command myself to you

Papiosa

I am truly unworthy of such an Angelic tribune as you and yet I thirst to know more, Come! For I can see that there is much for us to discuss along the way, no doubt you will make a good companion for one such as I

Ext: As Pablo the Immortal and Papiosa walked and talked together, they entered beyond the Soul Cages and into the underworld, Stefan and Josephine were saved, and Hark and Simeon returned to the abode of the Angels. Mercidiah and Kali Ma kept a vigilant watch on any forces that threatened their Earthly Motherhood, and then of course there was the mysterious voice that would come to reveal itself as Angelo Stiles.

Int: The day had come when Josephine gave birth to a child and from time to time the presence of Angel Hark watched over him from afar, but one day the time would come for him to dream and by now that day had drawn near, and one day in

the home of Stefan and Josephine Stiles once again began the dream of the angel babies.

Josephine Young

Hey Stefan can you check on Angelo?

Int: **Stefan cradles Angelo in his arms.**

Stefan Stiles

Angelo, my son, how are we doing today, do you wanna play a game of hide and seek, do you wanna?

Int: **Just then the shadow of an angel appears towering over them, it is the spirit of Hark the Herald Angel.**

Hark The Herald Angel

Stefan my son, wake up

ANGEL BABIES
THE FLIGHT OF AN ANGEL

The **Voice of the Comforter** Where does this dream of the Angel Babies begin and? How does it start? If there are no doubts in my mind then it always starts here, with me. I am the point of reference for the time being, this moment is the beginning of every awakening moment. There is only this, the lingering and transient motion in space and time, everything and everyone is relative to this, as I am to me and I am beside myself.

I am only for now in eternity and the mind's eye, So I am set free on the wings of a prayer and all that I encompass, I am not alone as the comforter guides me and in our understanding we are equally compatible in this truth, The inner voice of this world are mines to bear and they are all each and every one of them a thunderous murmur, embedded in this the heart of my mind, where one speaks for all, where all speak for themselves.

The comforter although this, the quietness of my silence, has the strongest force to truly guide me, it is only for this reason and this reason alone, as it is necessary for this the beginning of my first steps, to take flight and then and only then will the silence break, and I will begin to soar and take to the depths and the breath, the width and the heights of heaven, high above all else except the Earth which is deep below, along with the deepness that is beside the toils and the labors of mankind.

Like a force of nature I will listen to the breath of the dying, and the delivery of morning cries in an endless succession of births given to life, it will instruct my every bending, twisting and turning, my every will of thought, tutoring my glide to every desire inclined, I shall endeavor to search every part of my innermost being, its' dreaming and its' song, my soul unseen for the keeping as if I had to be hidden but did not hide. I will travel to the other side of my sleeping as thou awakened by the watching of my own spirit from a distant place that my soul has found, I will know where I am and where I am to be before this spirit of mine had noticed me in my own keeping, we shall hasten each one after the other, dancing intimately upon the elements of our constructs and desire.

There shall we be no more than we ought to be and we shall see the beauty of creation in all its' glory, and I shall speak to the mountain unyielding while swallowing the salt of the sea not drowning in its' undertow or overcast by its shadow nor shall its' bitterness be of sorrow to me.

The Comforter Speaks Of the Hosts of Heaven Look at these the people of the world and tell me what do you see, for each and every one of them has an angel and guardian host for their own keeping, they are watched over eternally day and night and night through till day, but who watches over them and why indeed do the hosts of heaven themselves need to be of a concern to us, when we in turn watch over them. Even as a defender of these the realms of humanity even you and I are desired and required to have someone watch over us, although we are not aware of the order of all things that prevail unseen by the living eye, you must remain aware that you are not of the order of the hosts of heaven, you are a defender of it, and so they cannot see you but hear you nor do they truly know of you existence, but bare you, yes there are others like you born into the infinite wars and laws of mankind and their eternal destiny which naturally rests with us and others like us, but your purpose is to serve the hosts the guardians of the Earth, and the will of the realm will concern itself with us, as its' keepers and defender.

If ever uncertain of the way, if ever unsure of the will, and if ever doubtful of the action to take the you must seek out a fellow servant and kindred soul who has the power of knowledge and the understanding to administer it to you in all proportions, and beyond all else to set about equal and fair display of every intention that is made ever present. His soul, his spirit is both young and old and his view is both narrow and short as much as it is wide and longstanding, his name is written as wisdom, and it is written on the hearts and minds of all that is great in human qualities, wisdom is a solitary figure and commands many cherubs in his service, he is nothing but everything all in one breath and sits at the edge of all reasoning, and is also unseen nor can he be found by anyone who is not seeking.

Wisdom is known to frequently habituate as an idyllic proclamation prophesying over the watchtower in this his domain, as a bearer of his foremother and so let it be known that wisdom is only in truth an observer, whose intentions is not to react in the usual regard as the hosts of heaven may appear to do so, nor does he sway with the opinionated revelations of the day or the night or the night through till day.

Regarding the hosts of heaven let it remain with us that if humankind is or are left unguarded for a moment in time, then this is the point that they are not only most vulnerable, but defenseless against Sheol and open to be preyed upon at any point in their natural lives even at an end to the making of their own divisive designs, of course this the cycle of their existence is interwoven with ours and it is this, our predisposition that has linked us to their realm and so the hosts are forever vigilante, and somewhat willingly in all practical portions in our honor and servitude, aware of how to best serve mankind as he is directed through this his natural life.

The more the hosts of heaven can influence and administer to each and every soul, the more the host is able to naturally guide and watch over him, until such appointed time has transpired or come to an end, It is the reason for our being that as defenders not to interfere but to witness, protect and influence in the same natural way as the hosts do and to do all else to guard the realm of heaven itself, In a way we are the intermediary's who purpose is to protect the protector and guard the guardian. The hosts of heaven cannot interfere in this matter nor change the course or destiny of mankind, although we are also inclined not to interfere in matters unconcerned with us.

This matter has always been considered as the most important relationship between mankind, their guardian angels and us the keepers of this realm simply because mankind and all living beings have a soul which is influenced by a spirit which is naturally influenced by the hosts.

Every host or guardian has a duty to fulfill albeit of a greater or lesser degree to the soul of man, and it is this relationship that is most valued, most sacred and above all else most honored within these realms, only in the depths of the abyss and the dwelling place of the un-living do we exchange one for the other when the soul is released and the spirit is renewed or united with the host.

It is only Sheol that we all watch, wait and look out for eternally, both coming and going in a motion unknown to any of its' kind, as every one of mankind when faced with this, the Angel of sheol is not aware that the hosts of heaven or his guardian has already prepared and made an agreement in exchange in this the grace of his soul.

An Exchange between Angel and Man As for mankind let it be duly noted that in this his legacy, and in this his long withstanding history, and in this his greatest desires, and in this his greatest ambitions and what he is, and what he was, and what he is to become will all be weighed up in this exchange. Sheol is the only spirit that moves among the living and the un-living. Even thou for some of us that are in the dwelling place of Sheol, let it be known that it is forbidden for any spirit to walk amongst the living or indeed on hallowed ground, although this is not so for the Angel of Sheol. As he above all else is free to move among us, and wherever he chooses to, and to exchange with whom so ever, any and every soul of mankind.

So why does Sheol continue to have a hold and a degree of power over humanity, it is simply that all things come to pass and all things come to an end, in Sheol the life of the soul is integral to us all, but man himself as he is, is not eternal, he is not forever, and nothing is more eternal that time, and time is no more than nothing, and Sheol is nothing more than a second in eternity and a moment in time.

For the sake of unnecessary torment, suffering and worry and regret let it be said that Sheol is not to be feared, nor should man himself be frightened to face an Angel of Sheol or the dwelling place that engages his soul, as this is the natural way of all things that come by this way as a pathway that was given through and over to us by him, in whom our belief, faithfulness and salvation and transformation is lived out through the sacrifice of the lamb of Yeshua.

The understanding of this and any task that is set before us, is only to fulfill the purpose of that which we are here to do, every need, every desire, every purpose however insignificantly intended must be carried out and must be fulfilled albeit through Earthly governance and proper understanding of this the utmost value that can be bestowed upon it, Time and time again mankind has failed to live up to his greatest expectations simply because his nature of the Earth pushes him to eagerly and overzealously fulfill his own undertaking, without the value and proper understanding that has been granted and laid upon his being.

Even for us to know the true nature of Yahweh we must first take account of the natural order of the world, and live out a simple and natural life however ordinary it may seem to be, as this the world is laid out before itself we must Endeavour to chart our course in and around it, taking note of mankind until such time has come to pass.

The truth being, that Yeshua has laid out before him a simple and practical life, and yet mankind stills struggles with his own will, not even truly knowing if he or she is indeed saved for what all that the hosts of heaven, have made preparation for.

Every generation passes through the threshold of this knowledge and understanding, and yet some still will not grasp the true teaching of this eventuality, when will he or she will see the face of God and what will take place and transpire in such a matter of great force and reckoning, none but themselves need to know, as it is written, that only one as just as himself can see his face **The View from a Cathedral** Anticipation strikes me from here, as to do the birds that give witness as they team across the sky like flocks in flight across the air, dark skies give way to the illuminations down below, allowing my beating wingspan to spread high and above the points of this monument, something that will always give way to those that seek its' offering.

The stars above appear brightly, flickering one by one underneath the earthly particles that pass throughout the night, I am content and satisfied for the moment as all is quiet, peaceful and well, but soon the winds will push me along as only they can, and

I like the earthly particles will brush along and pass the moonlit sky as a shadow still unknown.

If I am to take account of all and everything that is laid out before me then let me take account of myself as I am just as important and valuable in this moment of life as the next, and yet my significance here is nothing, here in this the creation of my own making, it was simply the light of a world shining intensely so bright that I could only see the infinite life of all souls flickering in its' beauty, and so upon the wings I soared with the true intentions of the heart, I could not settle, nor could I rest for there was no place in which I could stand if only for a moment, in every breath was just another view of something that was as of a dream unraveling.

If I came to a high place I would simply be still and wait until the winds or time itself had pushed me up and onward, if I felt to attend to a soul below I could not, for I knew that no soul had been forsaken and the hosts of heaven were there in my stead. The world was my concern but it did not call out to me for any reason, for any purpose, which was to serve it and all who dwelled there and yet I felt needed. For if I had thought to abandon my reason for being, then surely it would all just vanish and disappear and I would be there no more, I am here and here they are, just as much as they had been here before.

It felt like life knew me unknowingly and impersonally, the further away the horizon, the more bright the infinite star, as I hastened to chase the edge of the twilight where the moon would descend giving way to the Sun, I was suspended in an inner space and the event of time was beginning to elapse as if an eclipse could begin or indeed end at any moment of my flight, the wind with its' sweeping currents would carry me swiftly pushing me along up and over on toward the seas and the tide. However deep, and how ever solemn, the raging waters from beneath its' surface would find a way to emerge and beat against itself in as many ways as a vast uncontrollable eruption in motion, only to resettle and recoil in upon itself, and then repeating the action again, and again, capturing serenity in its bellowing and stirring torrent, from one rage to the next like a never ending boundless, vast, and wide open space.

The Comforter Returns After this feeling had been cast, no sooner than I had parted company with the comforter, I felt this solitude beside myself, although seemingly so was such a presence, with which was much more than just an empty space, there lingered a trace of his being, beginning in me a transcendental dream like the raging waters once calm. I was swiftly floating away, and it was by now a deafening scream from a silent desert, the harsh hollowing of a scarred and desolate place, a sea of sand dunes, which upon nothing was borne, there was nothing but I was aware that still you were there, and so on I flew until I knew nothing and no more.

Nothing more than the sound of my own heart, nothing more than the breath of my own being, the ceaseless endeavors unreached, but there you were calling to me from the deepest recesses of my soul until I fell.

Until love struck a blow as if the thundering snow clouds that hid the heavens had turned into rainclouds and had set upon me, striking lightning from high above the unknown and I began to fall, I was falling endlessly to my destiny, as if I were abandoned in my flight of stride and there lay before me and my own naked truth, now yielding to its' own. I was now within me and beside myself, and yet here was this the story that I had told, but where does it start, how will it begin, Sing Stefan sing, sing Hosanna to the King and Hark the Herald Angel will listen and you will know where I was to be, before the spirit had noticed you, we shall hasten each one after the other, dancing upon the constructs of our desire.

There shall we be no more than we ought to be, and I shall see the beauty of love in all its' glory and we shall speak to the mountains once again, if only to know that there is none greater both yielding and swallowing the salt of the seas, and it shall not be bitter or sorrowful to me for the comforter will know me but leave me as I am and as I ought to be, when the silence has softly spoken until it desires to inquire only to me, until it desires to inquire no more.

Wisdom speaks of Eternity I had come to fall down on my knees and found myself uttering a prayer beside myself locked within the thoughts of my mind, this was the moment that wisdom had arrived and descended upon me softly, breaking my fall in my stride of flight, but there you were once again attending to my every need, for this place in which I had come to dwell within, was a sanctuary for me and I knew that you were still there as a dear friend, showing me all the mercy that love could bestow upon me, accepting my every gratitude and thanksgiving for your precious presence in my company, when all along I thought I was all alone in my solitude.

The Comforter Speaks of Man There is within us a token of each other spanning the very nature of our innermost being, and it is through this thread that we are all bound, each one together, but most of all we are all brought into our own understanding and union through this, the beloved bright and morning star, that is to say that which he is and we are not, but if we are to be adored then it is because he is to be adored and if we are to be judged then it is simply because he is to be judged in our namesake.

None have been more loved than he, and all are called into question simply because he is, and because of him all are forgiven, simply because most of all he is the most adored.

Let his knowledge proceed from his being as a testimony that bears longevity, let his eyes bear witness to the beauty and imaginings of this world, if the task of restoration belongs to him, then let us find kindness and favor in his presence, for he has shouldered the weight and the burden if only to seek a place of love and peace and understanding with his brethren and his fellow man.

It is through him that we are brought into union and wise counsel through his endurance and long suffering, attentively attending to set down and establish an agreement with anyone seeking union with this the agreement between the servant of the lord, and the hosts of heaven.

For in his loneliness did I comfort him and in his ways did faith guide him, and in his dreams did you play host to guard over him, for each of us to know that if but one of us should abandon him he will never be alone.

His debt is with us as he has always sought to make a way for himself despite the ways of the world that forever trouble him, both the day through to night and the night through until day. Even when they know not, who unseals the dictates of their day, he shall be pleased not to take account of his own works as we are all servants in the name of love, and for this being we shall work accordingly to deliver him to his rightful salvation. Within this is the message of humanity that none of us shall put ourselves above the other but to ensure that each other is administered to and cared for.

Within him there are many unwritten sermons and they are unto us handed down as gifts, each one manifesting itself into a blessing from heaven itself, the receiver are those who shall Endeavour to walk and live in this, the light of his life.

The Leap to Faith I now knew of the will to fly, I had been summoned to its' calling at the bridge at the edge of the watchtower, it was to serve to me as a reminder and remembrance of those who had flown out of these heavens before, never to return.

Little by little we gave way to an account, little by little we knew less of ourselves, but more assuredly of what was to come and what was to come to pass, and why we were now to surpass every self desire and to do away with and overcome our every ambition, to give ourselves over and to put everything else in its' stead.

I could see the lives of the un-living in Sheol as they were and had been before, the numbers were mounting, and we were being counted as each other's sound gave way to a number, until singles grew into multiples, until multiples grew and gave way to the countless.

And so even if the world were plunged into darkness, and no one could see the signs, as I had seen them or as I had witnessed them, then who among you if not I would find a light to shine amidst the fear, and if only for one living soul would give cause to a way and allow this love to shine so brightly then surely the hosts of heaven would bless them, allowing us to fulfill our ambitions, if only to protect and defend them throughout the ages of time.

On Earth when a beautiful soul dies the whole world becomes filled with a heartfelt emptiness and sorrow, although in this loss there is much to gain because in heaven, when a beautiful soul is born this can only be the beginning of something new and wonderful.

An Earth Mothers Awakening There they stood as we all would, defending the hosts of heaven, face to face with the Angel of Sheol in the midway of the heavens, in this the resting place, where a sea of souls lay beside the amethyst glare of a rusting red heat rising out of their ashes. Wisdom one hundred and forty one thousand, humanity one hundred and forty two thousand, the comforter one hundred and forty three thousand and me, one hundred and forty four thousand.

As I looked outwardly and beyond I could see us high in ascension, going forth between the opposite polar stars, some of us took to go in different directions, I knew this would be the last time that we would fly in stride as one prevailing flock, not yet worthy of man, not yet prepared to sing our deliverance to the face of God.

This the vision of a place, here where time stood still and quiet, and kept a reflection in its' beauty, my eyes had laid itself upon the wonders of this our heavenly creation, and then there came to me in its' appearance, a starlit shining as if it had set itself before me in recognition and guidance, be it to my death or onto ward my revelation and destiny leading.

If the words of this heart of this mind were unknown to me before, then this was the time for them to come forth and to sing and reveal anew, never had I questioned the why or wherefore, never had I felt such almighty surrender, but it knew my name by name and it knew me by my nature. From day through till night, from night through till day, from birth unto life, from life unto death and from death until dust, Follow me, follow your nature, come see the creation of your destiny, follow me, follow your nature wherefore your comforter leads you.

As I leapt the leap of faith the glare had ceased to be and Sheol was no more to me, in its' stead there by the towering cathedral stood a solitary figure praising and begging for forgiveness upholding his will in her majesty's name, on her knees praising only by the nature that knows her, there as I stood over her kneeling, this was my mother that had given life to my seed.

Stefan's Destiny Is Revealed As the singing fades to silence and the song is heard no more there lays the way to the fate of the befallen Angels crucified by the spikenards, fulfilling the prophecy of the last harvest of those that shall stand side by side with the lamb on the Day of Judgment. Stefan's' eyes now give way to a stillness in time as the starlit shining persists' no more, his celestial body covering the breadth of a cornerstone, here in this place where he is to remain as a keeper and a watcher overtime as his heart beats its' pulse into the Earth and as his soul becomes one with the generations that shall surpass him into the wilderness of the world beyond

ANGEL BABIES

JOSEPHINE STILES

Int: The Sun is moments away from stetting into the evening of a twilight sky, two figures a young boy and his mother are slowly approaching a hill on the southern edge of a Low Fell in England.

Eventually they both come to stand silently still as they have come to gaze at this majestic and monumental figure, known to the locals of this town as the Angel Of The North.

The child is eagerly excited and begins running around race fully and playfully encircling the ground that holds the stature firmly in its place, his mother is almost entranced as she looks around at this vast landscape through the eyes of resolve and contemplation, images of the past run violently through her mind, calling out to her memories, as she looks upwardly imagining what everything looks like from the dizzy heights of the Northern Angels eyes.

For a moment she is alone in her thoughts and her feelings, while the child has absently absconded and strayed from her external view, she pays no attention to the winds that whisper in the air, nor does she feel the enveloping cold air, that sets about her somewhat vulnerable and timid frame, as solitary as the figure that beholds her in suspense, for now time is a place that could be anywhere but nowhere to hear her whispers.

EXT: Josephine speaks her mind in the presence of the statue for the winds to force them to reach out to Stefan.

Josephine Stiles

Its' the red sky at night that mostly gets me, I always
thought to come here one day, to think, to feel and
to remember, and now that I'm here it conjures up all
kinds of emotions, I know that somehow you can hear
me, see me, feel me. It's silly really I know, and so
many times I imagine that so many of us have seen
the signs around us, but in these symbolic monuments
there is nothing that can be of comfort to me now...

...lead me not into temptation, but have I? Baby please don't
do this to me now, I can't take it anymore, this pain its'
hurting me now, so much more, and I don't know what to do"

Ext: She pauses & sighs.

Everything that I am now, all that I encompass and embrace
is as its meant to be that much I know, from the very
beginning of our time together up until now, as if our
dreams through your life has shaped me and completed my
being, I read all the tell tale signs, I do, I do, I really
do I study the stars and the sacred teachings, I'm transfixed
in the scriptures and their hidden meaning's... ...giving me
purpose, giving purpose to others while hiding my own truth
from those that cannot begin to understand the severity
and the importance that lies out there in front of me.

Ext: She looks ahead while leaning to one side of the statue.
Only in my deepest dreams do I see you as you were, as
we both were, as you are now, always living in my life as
something inside of me, and I know as silly as it sounds its
true Stefan, it's true, I've been touched by an Angel and that
Angel is you, but beyond that I've also been loved by one

**Ext: She falls to her knees and cries attempting to wipe away
each tear as it develops, one after the other.**
So what more can a girl even hope to ask for, if not
for something as so precious and as inspiring as all of
this, and even as my life has been with you, one eventful

moment to the next, I know that one day you will either
come to me or that I will surely go to where you are

**Ext: She's gets up from her knees, much more certain, determined
and stronger in spirit.**

I pray not the hour Stefan! But I do command
it, with every beat of my heart

**Ext: Just then she is panicked and looks frantically around for
the boy, as she gazes up to the Angel Of The North, and she
sees her child delicately, diligently, tippy toeing along
the wingspan of the sculpture, as she shouts up to him.**

ANGELO! Come down from there

ANGEL BABIES
THE FIRE FLIGHT OF DESIRE

Ext: Imagine that you have woken up in a place that was once a
bustling town or a city, or a living metropolis, full of
life inhabited, by souls, full of love and laughter, and
then now try to forget that after wars and plagues and
disease and neglect and waste, what is left behind in this
dark and dense shallow place, if only the empty echoes
of nothing more than death , and where else is there
to wander amongst these forgotten ruinous wastelands of
yesteryear, as you remain lost within this world of ghostly
structures, and decaying, dilapidated buildings, amongst
these somewhat defaced and broken statues, that have come
to serve and stand as representations and monuments of
a distant land from a bygone age, now resigned to your
deepest memories, and when you have forgotten all of this,
only then shall you remember that once there was a place
called oblivion.

Ext: Somewhere in oblivion amongst the fallen and the ruinous
place of an underworld.

As the singing fades to silence and the song is heard no more
there lays the way to the fate of the befallen Angels, crucified
by the spikenards, fulfilling the prophecy of the last harvest,
of those that shall stand side by side with the lamb on the day
of judgment. Stefan's' eyes now give way to a stillness in time
as the starlit shining persists' no more, his celestial body

covering the breadth of a cornerstone, here in this place where he is to remain as a keeper and a watcher overtime as his heart beats its' pulse into the Earth and as his soul becomes one with the generations that shall surpass him into the wilderness of the world beyond.

Ext: We hear the voice of Stefan speaking with a stranger amidst the darkness of oblivion.

Stefan Stiles

Once I was something of concern to a lot of very special and important people, my life was not just ordinary, it was the amazement of the heavens and much more than that, I have seen beyond the wonders of the mortal soul into the heart of the universe, this beginning was only a moment that pushed me and all that I love and hold dear to me, to its' very limit, something much more than I would naturally dare to understand and now I am left to wander, to watch, to pause, to think and to feel all the great and wonderful but beneath that, I am beneath the lowly and the forgotten, and you like me are trapped, in an oblivion with the unimaginable pain and loss of all that I could and would have been, if for a moment, I would been what I was and not what I am and have become.

Ext: The character extends his hand holding an empty tin cup.

Flea

Place a nickel in my cup stranger and I shall
reveal to you the very answer to the question that
troubles you, even though you truly have no troubles
at all, just a nickel my friend, just a nickel

Stefan Stiles

A nickel?

Flea

A nickel would do

Stefan Stiles

But I don't have a nickel

Flea

Fool! You dare to tell me that you, who have held the
world as your possession, but you do not hold about you
a single nickel in your possession, Fool! Fool! Fool

Ext: Stefan looks down upon the lowly scrawny figure of a man.

Stefan Stiles

Who are you?

Flea

We've been here before, but to you and this one, this
is the abode of the heartless ones, I am the Flea.

Stefan Stiles

The Flea! What kind of name is that?

Flea

Don't you remember, I always remember, this cup
that the history man gave to me, he said, a man
should never thirst, but I always thirst, like
the history man I thirst for knowledge

Stefan Stiles

The history man! What history?

Flea

The thing is when I was a child, I got beat about my head,
I've never seen no doctor, so now I have to stutter, I was
expecting to make a dollar today, they say the history
man may be coming soon, I don't know for sure but at
least a nickel would fill my cup and quench my thirst

Stefan Stiles

Flea!

Flea

Its' the name that I bare, coz I sticks too you like
fleas' on a dog, although it gives reference to nothing,

coz they're aint' no dogs around here, other than
a problem, one of which I do believe you have

Stefan Stiles

So what is the flea going to do for me, because I don't
believe that for one second you can truly undo my doing?

Flea

Fool! Fool! Fool with a mind possessed of foolishness,
and a foolish nature and no heartbeat towards the ones,
that would even bare a tear to cry, and yet you speak
of loss and abandonment, that surely would mean or
suggest that you had, or have a heart full of emotions,
who knows even a whisper of love, wouldn't you say?

Stefan Stiles

Flea, what does it matter to you, of how I
am of design, or construct or depth?

Flea

Because in their world we would possess all these
things and more, like you said, but in this world
we are found with less are less fortunate, and
found with wanting more than we can possess

Stefan Stiles

That's true

Flea

Nothing is truer, come! We shall descend and inquire upon
the oblivious wreckers of life, if you are pleasing to
them, then they shall reward you, and you in turn you shall
reward me with a nickel, and I shall answer the question
to the one who would hold the world in its' possession

**Ext: Stefan and Flea begin to move among the shadows of
oblivion.**

Flea

They've been existing here for a long, long, long time,
so long in fact they can't remember when, but what's the
use of them remembering, what good can come out of this
and that, in this ere' place, only thing good about it,
is the history man, he be a good, good, good friend of
mine, and that's another reason why I have my cup

Stefan Stiles

The history man, who is the history man?

Flea

I'll be collecting every nickel and dime just to make a
dollar, sure as hell makes for a good payment for thirsty
work, nothing like the history man to make you forget
all your worries if only for little while, they say that
if you be of interest, of high and mighty qualities,
then you can be of use to the history man, that's why I
be collecting every nickel and dime in this ere cup

Stefan Stiles

But that's just an empty tin cup

Flea

I see that you're even lost to your own eyes, and to
what salvation did it bring you, come let us enter
into this place of the past, who knows maybe it will
restore your sight and allow you to see again

**Int: As they both entered into a darkened old ruinous building,
there were many broken discarded and disheveled souls to
see them enter within, an old woman was quick to approach
them first.**

Old Woman

Is this him, is that him, not much to look at is he?

Flea

No! No! No! This is not him

Old Woman

Then kill him, he's no good to us in ere' is he

Flea

This one is for the history man, he represents nothing, and only wishes and speaks of a mortal love, he cannot be killed

Old Woman

No! Well we'll see about that, I'll cut him from ear to ear with a twisted blade, and then he'll bleed for sure

Int: The old woman pulls out a rusty old curled up knife and stabs at the waist side of Stefan, laughing out loud and cackling at the same time but Stefan doesn't even flinch, she the shrieks with shock and surprise.

Flea

He cannot bleed old woman

Old Woman

What is he, immortal then?

Flea

Near enough, he's the reason why we are ere' but he don't know nothing, not a thing, not a single thing

Int: Another of the spectators stands up to look and inquire at the spectacle of their new guest.

Spectator

He's a watcher, or a guardian, or something like that, isn't he

Old Woman

Let me rip his heart out, that'll kill him for sure

Int: Just then all the broken discarded and disheveled souls stand up and Flea and Stefan are surrounded by the crowd who are by now looking very menacing.

Flea

No! No! No! Let the history man decide his fate

Spectator

The history man, that's if he ever turns up

Old Woman

Well if we can't kill him, what can we do with him then?

Spectator

Baptize him

The Crowd

Yeah! Baptize him in fire

Old Woman

He'll never burn, he's far too pure for that,
bet I'll find a way, I'll get him for sure

Flea

Look! You shouldn't provoke him, at least show me
some gratitude, after all I brought him here, but
not for the likes of you to do away with him

Old Woman

Gratitude, for what, it is him then isn't it, its' him
and them others that brought put us ere', he should show
us some gratitude and die, coz I'd sooner kill him dead
if it were possible, c'mon then show us his wings

Spectator

He ain't got no wings

Int: Someone in the crowd shouts

I bet he wish he had

**Int: The flea pulls Stefan to one side and prompts him to manifest
himself in order to satisfy the crowd.**

119

Flea

Ok! Ok! Whose gonna be the first to hand over
a tidy handsome fee to see his wings?

**Int: The crowds begin to gather around closing in the margins
between themselves and the Flea and Stefan.**

Spectator

I'll give you a nickel

Spectator 2

I'll give you a dollar, and nickel

Old Woman

I'll give you two dollars, if I see a pair of wings

Flea

Done! My friend, the question of resolve
is at hand, do you agree?

Stefan Stiles

Agree to what, these people are the damned are they not?

Flea

There you go again, Accusing! Accusing! Accusing,
were all damned in ere, even you my foolish friend,
damned if we do and damned if we don't so to speak,
especially if you don't show them something majestic!

Stefan Stiles

But…!

Flea

But nothing, look there

Stefan Stiles

Where, look where?

Flea

There through the window across the time of
passage and tell me what you see?

Stefan Stiles

I see nothing, except the horizon, lit up like a glowing light

Flea

Yes! Yes! Yes you see it lit up but can you reach it

Stefan Stiles

What do you mean?

Flea

Well you see to me and these low life's, its' the border, its'
a shattered hope, a false dream and who knows maybe even an
illusion, but it's also the border of life and death, which
no man, woman or beast or Angel or otherwise can reach, even
if you flew toward it in a thousand lifetimes with the might
of heaven behind you, you would never ever reach it, and
yet we can dwell here in all eternity, and see it as clearly
as if it were already here, and we were already there

Stefan Stiles

Maybe so, but what will my actions merit me?

Flea

It will merit you nothing except shall we say two
dollars and who knows, but that's more than enough to
answer all your questions a hundred times over, you
do remember my friend don't you, you do remember?

Stefan Stiles

Ok! I shall do it

Flea

Wait! A minute, Wait! Just a minute, at least let me set
the stage for you… And now my friends for the first time
beneath these walls of degradation and ruin, a sign, for
the seasons, the accuser and the damned, for the wreckers

and the wreck less, for the sinful unrepentant souls, I present to you, the most magnificent and majestic scene of our trying times, the wings...of an Angel, Now my friend Now!

Int: Just then Stefan willed his wings to appear and just as soon as was said, they did appear, unfolding from the seal of his spine with his back outstretching and yawning wide, opening in all its' glory and splendor, like a beautiful display of a stunning showpiece, like the feathers of a peacock in bloom for all the crowd and flea to witness and behold, but then suddenly in the midst of the bewilderment, shock and surprise the old woman pushed through the crowd of spectators and shouting, shrieking and screaming.

Old Woman

Burn them! Burn his wings, cut them off! Destroy them

Int: Just then she struck a flame and set upon Stefan and sure enough his wings did ignite into flames much to his own surprise, the crowd all rushed out of harm's way as the scorching inferno of flames threw and fell their way, the crowd looked on in horror as Stefan let out his birth cry piercing through their bleeding ears somewhat like a dolphin screaming for life, with such a severe and penetrating sound that could be heard on the distantly lit horizon, and by none other than the Angel of Justice, who in that very moment suddenly appeared like an mighty expansion of light shooting through from the horizon, appearing in the very room to see the burning flames now consuming the wings on Stefan's back.

Angel Of Justice

Stop this! Stop this at once

Ext: By now Stefan's wings had been consumed and there was by now not single trace of their awesome beauty, but instead there was only a skeletal frame where his pride and strength use to be. As the Flea approached the angel of justice, a young boy of teenage years placed two dollars at Stefan's feet which had fallen out of the old woman's hands, Stefan had hardly noticed him, unlike the angel of justice.

Angel Of Justice

The buying of souls within is prohibited,
to whom does this money belong?

Flea

To no one, its' for nothing

Angel Of Justice

Or for freedom, perhaps

Old Woman

Yes! Yes for freedom

Angel Of Justice

Commanded by who?

Flea

By no one

Angel Of Justice

For hope I believe

Spectator

Yes! For hope

Angel Of Justice

Who is the strange one in question?

Flea

I do not know him, a capturer of captives,
perhaps, a strange one indeed your majesty

Angel Of Justice

Rise my fallen fellow, explain and justify yourself

**Int: Stefan stood to his feet and Flea fell silent and retreated
back quite quickly into the crowd, while quickly grabbing
the two dollars placed at Stefan's feet, just then a darkly
figure appeared through the smoldering smoke screen amidst**

the confusion, it was the history man also known in other
parts of the realm as Papiosa.

Angel Of Justice

I should have known you were here Papiosa, a servant of time,
tell me who is he to you, and what do you want with him?

Papiosa

If permitable, he is mine already, if I can truly satisfy
and justify my claim on his pitiful disposition

Angel Of Justice

The question is, can you?

Flea

I was asked by his gracious and noble one too...

Angel Of Justice

To what?

Flea

To acquire, the smitten one's trust and
hand him over to the history man

Angel Of Justice

For what! Two dollars?

Flea

No! Your majesty, for a nickel

Angel Of Justice

I see, is this true?

Papiosa

It is, and if you don't mind your majesty, but justice
must be seen to be done, don't you agree?

Angel Of Justice

I did not permit you to add your opinion
to this understanding, what do you seek
with this one so importantly so?

Papiosa

To conclude a terrible chapter your gracious one, he has
no more use to you or anyone now, he's already amongst
the forgotten, all but a memory to his own name and his
father's legacy, a mere tale to the teller, let him enter
the into the soul cages to rest and sleep in peace"

Angel Of Justice

With you as his keeper no doubt, The one who cages souls
until it reverts back to its' infancy or its' original
state as before time of conception, allowing it to
sleep until all traces of its inherited and inhabited
experience has transmigrated so it in turn you can
manipulate the use of this knowledge to acquire insights
of your own, no I shall not, Rise my fallen fellow

Int: Stefan walks toward the angel of justice.

Angel Of Justice

What say you to your justice?

Stefan Stiles

I don't understand

Angel Of Justice

Then there be naught else, but reality

Stefan Stiles

Reality, But, but you're a woman

Angel Of Justice

For that insult alone I should leave you to your destined fate

Stefan Stiles

Forgive me, for my remark but, but I have never seen

Int: The onlookers laugh out loud.

Angel Of Justice
Be Silent, you have never seen what?

Int: Flea whispers to Stefan.

Flea
The Angel Of Justice

Stefan Stiles
I have never seen nor given witness to what
I all but thought, did not exist

Angel Of Justice
But I do, so there

Papiosa
As you can see my majesty, he is rude and ignorant as well
as overly used and illiterate as well as exhausted, he's
quite literally burnt out, his needs are no more, allow
me to draw a quick conclusion to this matter of counsel

Angel Of Justice
I shall be the one to draw conclusions and
give counsel, from where does he come?

Flea
The other world your majesty, almost half breed
angel and human hereditary, but not nearly

Angel Of Justice
Human! Human herediatary, I have never
seen nor known such things

Stefan Stiles
That's what I was trying to tell you, how come we never
met before, don't you think it a little strange?

Angel Of Justice

But if this is all true, then we are all
each one of us in separate worlds

Stefan Stiles

That's not entirely true but I can see why you would
look at it that way, your reasoning is just, but the
truth is you've just never been there before

Angel Of Justice

I see you have humor to match, especially in
the face of adversity, how very noble

Papiosa

He's finished your justice, barely a fool, let him have the
two dollars to pay the Flea for the truth of his deliverance

Angel Of Justice

I see no deliverance, among the wretched actions of your
perpetrators and divisive doing, I see my justice is
required, but for the plea of you Papiosa, is there not a
bargain you won't consider, amongst these lost and condemned
manifestations seeking a way to be rid of even you if they
could, is there no camaraderie here amongst demon or devil,
for those of you who are truly sorry, what shall you have me
do now, but for those of you who are not, you shall thirst
but never quench, and so it shall be unforgivably so

**Int: The crowds begin to mumble and murmur amongst
themselves.**

The Crowd

We are sorry your majesty, we are so very sorry
your benevolent one, grant us your mercy

Angel Of Justice

Then Sing! Sing it out loud, Sing it so that it echoes
throughout the walls of your dungeons, sing it so it
carries a song across the ages of time and opens the
gate to your hearts and minds, Sing! Sing! Sing!

Papiosa

I can see some things never change

Angel Of Justice

And why should they, when I do not see you opening
any of the cages that you are so hasty to close

Flea

Your majesty, what shall I do with the two dollars?

Angel Of Justice

Hand it to me

Int: Flea looks at Papiosa.

Papiosa

Give it to her

Int: Flea hands her the money.

Angel Of Justice

Now extend your tin cup to me

Int: Flea holds out his cup.

Angel Of Justice

Two dollars for the truth, will it be enough?

**Int: She drops the money into the cup and as soon as it rattles
and jingle jangles in the bottom of the cup, it disappears
and vanishes into thin air.**

Angel Of Justice

Now come, come, what did you expect, a miracle, nothing lasts
forever, but a human Angel, that's different, something's
will have to change, but first I want to kiss him

Papiosa

No! No! Definitely not! This is not the way of things,
forgive me but don't do this, I forbid it

Angel Of Justice
Forbid, who do you think you are talking
too, Stefan come to me

Papiosa
No! Stefan, she will kill you for sure

Angel Of Justice
If he is human as you say he is, then yes he will die, but if
he is not, I shall reward him handsomely, come to me Stefan

Int: **Stefan walks to the standing place of the angel of justice,
as she will fully commands her wings to appear embracing
him into her bosom, shadowing his burnt out skeletal frame
until he is completely wrapped up in her all encompassing
concealment.**

Angel Of Justice
You are truly beautiful, how I have ever found such
an immortal sacrifice, is beyond me, kiss me and
remember me, for I am your saving grace, die and
forget me, and I shall hold you forever to my bosom

Int: **As they began kissing, the skeletal wings began to crack
and break away from Stefan's body, even as the angel of
justice tightened her embrace, deepening her innermost
intentions into feelings and emotion, penetrating into
and beyond Stefan's heart and mind, as her wings gently
nurtured and naturally unfolded forming around him, the
angel of justice was affectionately amused by Stefan's
charming and appealing character. The crowds were also
surprised to see that Stefan still withstood the moment of
their embrace.**

The Crowd
He lives!

Angel Of Justice
Yes he lives

Int: Just then the old woman who had beset upon Stefan stepped out of the crowd trembling and cowering with fear.

Old Woman

I'm sorry your justice, please, please forgive
me for my crime of vengeance, forgive us all
for our tormented fears of conviction

Ext: Then as she tried to weep, she could not find it inside herself to summon the tears of remorse.

Stefan Stiles

I forgive you woman

Angel Of Justice

You there!

Old Woman

Me?

Angel Of Justice

Reward him

Old Woman

How, with what your majesty, I have not the
means to put right what I have done?

Angel Of Justice

With your heart, you shall set about
putting it right, if you have one

Old Woman

With my heart, but how?

Angel Of Justice

Then you are of no use to me now, I think that
you should perish amongst the debris and the
ashes of your own doing and be no more

Old Woman

Is this is to be my fate, then so be it

Stefan Stiles

She knew not anything of justice, let her be

Angel Of Justice

She knew to take away your wings Stefan

Old Woman

If I could, I would return them to him, if I could I would

Stefan Stiles

She was provoked, as were the others, allow her your mercy

Angel Of Justice

They knew not of mercy to baptize you with fire

Old Woman

Please your gracious one, if I could put out the fires of desire I would, I would surely do that with all my heart

Angel Of Justice

Then give him wings of fire

Old Woman

But how, I have no power

Angel Of Justice

Flea, hold out your cup

Int: Flea extends his empty tin cup toward the angel of justice.

Ext: Now while this incident was taking place unbeknown to Stefan, another Angel was hovering high above in the shadowy skies of oblivion, a winged figure of a creature, concealing a bow, as if in anticipation of the unfolding events of the trial and the judgment of Stefan Stiles now being conducted by the Angel of Justice.

Angel Of Justice
How much for the wings of fire?

Int: Flea begins to tremble almost frightened by the request.

Flea
I do believe the fee has already been
redeemed in kind your gracious one

Angel Of Justice
Good, let it be done, wings of fire for
the one descended of humans

**Int: No sooner had the Angel of justice finished speaking, than
this moment Stefan's back began to perforate with a blood
the color of a blue liquid flame, where his wings once were
and as it streamed red to blue and from blue to flames,
which grew and grew and then finally blazing into wings of
fire, meanwhile they had all scattered outside to see the
Bastion hovering in the skies above.**

Angel Leoine
This arrow bears your destiny, follow it through to the
horizon and beyond toward the future, and whatever happens,
and whatever you believe, and whatever you face, do not be
afraid, for your future and your destiny shall be rewritten
according to this revelation and the truth of the unwritten
laws of creation, now go through and prepare to fly with
courage, for your love of humanity depends upon it, fly south
to the sea of souls, for the one who awaits, these wings will
burn as long as there is a light shining in her heart for
you, if and when you find your passage way through the sea
of souls, you shall find your way home, be gone now, while
I think of how best to deal with these forsaken infidels

**Ext: And as soon as the bow was plucked and the arrow had been
sent and took aim and was sent hurtling into the distance
by the Sentient Bastion still hovering in the sky, known
only to some as Angel Leoine, very soon afterward Stefan
was airborne amidst the skies of oblivion in pursuit of the
now flaming arrow, that would eventually lead him through**

and beyond the eternal horizon and unknowingly toward his fate and ultimate destiny awaiting.

Ext: As Stefan set out to fly south, all the memories of his entire life flashed like images in front of his eyes, flooding into his veins swelling with energy, resounding and pushing upon his will, as he was now re-awakening and empowering his mind, his feelings and his emotions, surging with new life waking his soul and strengthening his love for none other than that of his beloved Josephine Stiles.

Ext: A middle aged woman is on her way to an airport somewhere in the U.S.A, to catch her flight on route to the U.K. her name is Mercidiah also an known as the Earth Mother who consummated her love with Angel Simeon giving birth to Angel Haven, Whom she gave up to become an Immortal amongst the decree of Empyreans. She is also a dear and trusted friend and of Josephine Stiles who consummated her love with Stefan giving birth to Angel Angelo.

Cab Driver
So what's this a summer vacation or sumpthin?

Mercidiah
Well yes, you could say that

Cab Driver
I've never been to England before, what's it like over there?

Mercidiah
Cold I guess, but it's my first visit as well

Cab Driver
What! You got relatives over there or sumpthin?
Mercidiah Well yes, I guess you put it that way, although I like to think of her as being more like a daughter

Cab Driver
A Daughter! No shit, what with grandchildren and everything?

Mercidiah
You certainly ask a lot of questions, for a Cab Driver

Cab Driver
I'm just inquisitive lady, I guess, I got a daughter
too you know, she's married, two kids, they're kinda
like angels, yeah the two of em' just like angels

Mercidiah
Is that right?

Cab Driver
You know I never really thought of it like that, I guess I
never really got pass just being a father, until she gave
birth, now look at me, already a gran daddy, sure makes my
life one big inquisitive question, I mean where do we go
from here, and that's what I keep asking myself, Oh! Well
anyway were here, so ere' do you need a hand with anything?

Mercidiah
No thank you, I'm fine, I can take it from here

Cab Driver
Well yeah! Have a nice day lady, and have a good
trip as well, England! Can you believe it

Mericidiah
You too friend and thank you

**Ext: As Mercidiah prepares for her flight, it is also late night
in a small town house just outside London. Josephine Stiles
is asleep in her bedroom while in the adjacent room her
teenage son, Angelo is also sleeping and deeply dreaming,
something of a re-occurring theme, something of which he
has been dreaming since his early childhood. The boy is
distressed and restless locked into the disturbances of a
nightmare, with flashes of lightning and thunderous storms
rolling forth throughout the heavens. Suddenly Angelo wakes
up in a cold sweat, shocked by the visions in his dream.**

Angelo Stiles

The sky is on fire, the sky, the sky's, burning

Int: Just then his mother, Josephine, enters the room as she has done before in the past and sits as Angelo's bedside

Josephine Stiles

Angelo darling, what's wrong

Angelo Stiles

Its' happening again, the whole world, its' like
it's all in flames, the sky and everything

Josephine Stiles

It's Ok! Angelo its' only a dream

Int: Josephine walks over to the window and pulls back the blinds, the moonbeams appear in the window, striking a bright silver light into the room.

Josephine Stiles

See Angelo, look, there's nothing there, there's nothing to be
afraid off, the sky is calm, everything is peaceful, I'm sure
your just thinking too much about stuff, like the doctor said

Angelo Stiles

But, I don't think about stuff like that mom, I don't read
about it, I just see it and I can feel it, its' like I know
sumphin's about to happen, I've seen things and I can't
explain it yet, not to you, not to anyone, but its' like
I've been there before, or like it knows that I know stuff

Josephine Stiles

Well whatever it is, we'll both deal with it together,
just remember I'm here for you as well, and I don't want
my baby to feel alone, or unloved or unappreciated, just
you remember that next time you go through stuff

Ext: Early in the morning Josephine is rushing around the house looking for her car keys, as soon as finds them in her

handbag, she quickly hurries and ushers Angelo into the car, who by now is very placid with a blank non expression on his face, the car pulls out from the drive on route to the airport to pick up Mercidiah. Later when they arrive at the airport, Mercidiah has disembarked and is at the arrivals point as Josephine pulls up in the car to pick her up. For a moment they kiss and embrace one another, before getting back into the car.

Mercidiah
Josephine, I can't quite believe it, My! My!
Look at you and Angelo, how wonderful to see
you both, I can see you've grown some too

Int: Angelo who is by now unconcerned and looking lost, looks up at Mercidiah and then gazes out of the car window, immediately Mercidiah becomes concerned.

Mercidiah
Is everything Ok Josey?

Josephine Stiles
Well no, not exactly

Mercidiah
What is it Josephine, what's wrong?

Josephine Stiles
Angelo's been having strange dreams, nightmares even,
I can't quite understand what it all means, I think
they may be premonitions or visions of some kind

Mercidiah
Premonitions, of what exactly, have you
seen any signs to confirm this?

Josephine Stiles
No! That's just it I haven't but I know, it's not
good, I think we should talk about it at length
later on, once Angelo has rested properly

Mercidiah

Don't be alarmed dear, premonitions are not out
of the ordinary where we are concerned, in fact
they're quite a natural and normal phenomenon

Josephine Stiles

I hope so

Mercidiah

Of course Josey' of course

Ext: Somewhere between oblivion and the sea of souls, Stefan is
now flying with the wings of fire, with a passionate will of
determined desire to push back the murky, muddy, darkened
depths like a tsunami preparing to unleash its' wrath upon
the unsuspecting creatures beneath, whipping up a torrent
now rising up into the treacherous blackened skies above,
like a fountain of fury disturbing the sea of souls in
their sudden cry and the awakening of none other than
the angel of the abyss, and the depths below, now rising
out of the sea of souls, shimmering like a watery diamond
with the souls of the lost and the damned, all sea like
and translucently formless in its' appearance of something
glistening, like liquid mercury born out of an anger that
rages both empty and endless, consuming all in its path as
though nothing ever could.

Angel Of The Abyss

You cannot change the laws of creation, son of Hark, nor
can you undo the depths of the abyss, your presence here
shakes the very sands of the bottomless sea's these wings
of fire that you possess are a curse and a judgment to
me, your every trial will cause the Earth to shake from
within and upon itself, have you no concern of what will
happen once you arrive to the other world, all shall be
endangered by the very justice you so carelessly flap and
fly with, so long as you have these wings I cannot permit
you to pass, think of your loved ones and spare them this
quest for mortal love, instead join me and come to know the
belly of the soulless sea's deep beneath, let me douse the
flames and put an end to this endless passion for desire

Stefan Stiles

I have been released and freed from my own doing, I have been granted another chance and it is by this clemency of exoneration that is mines to bare and mine alone, for if I am released from the boundless depths of oblivion, then I have also freed those with whom have felt that I held them captive for so very long and no doubt if a judgment is to be passed then let me fly homeward as each of us must eventually come to rest in a place that echoes and reflects a peace from within, I cannot hold the world in contempt for something it knows not of itself, nor can these flames be put out by a tempestuous sea that is drowning in its own sorrow

Angel Of The Abyss

Then I bid you farewell and good luck but don't say that I didn't warn you, for your wrath upon us may be a judgment unsurpassable, if you do not comprehend what it is you know not of yourself

Stefan Stiles

I know this much and I am not yet satisfied with the toils of my struggle and plight

Angel Of The Abyss

Then listen well for in the mountains that stand before you, I must warn you that as vast as they are and as wide as I am and yet still they do not bow to the treacherous sea of souls below, but little by little and spec by spec even they shall eventually crumble and fall piece by piece like the dust in these sands that are now scattered beneath me, even unto me the seas I am patient and I am just for I know in time they will crumble and fall to me

Stefan Stiles

You may be assured of one thing my friend but I cannot wait around to see what stories time has to tell, as we may all very well yield to you in time and you may be superior in these midst, but as for now the mountains still stand albeit of stubborn rock and stone

Angel Of The Abyss

Stubborn!" stubborn rock and stone, you amuse me,
maybe you should go and see the one who pulls down
the rigid rock from its' high and mighty places, for
it is only I who has truly seen the mountain move

**Int: As Josephine, Angelo and Mercidiah arrive home, Mercidiah
is anxious to know the details of Angelo's vivid dreams if
not nightmares. Angelo enters the room.**

Mercidiah

Angelo, I know you've probably been asked this question a
dozen times before but can you tell me any if everything
you can remember about your dreams since they started

Angelo Stiles

Why can't you tell her, unless you already have,
anyway its' all jumbled up, might not even be real

Josephine Stiles

But you've seen things haven't you, things that you
can't explain to me, maybe if you explain it to
merci she can help you to make sense of it all

Angelo Stiles

Well what do you wanna know, I don't know where or
how to explain it, I just see things that's all,
sometimes I can feel it, like I'm really there

Mercidiah

Ok! I can understand and appreciate that, but just tell
me what the feelings look like, and hopefully I can help
you to put them into some kind of sensible meaning,
something which I'm good at and could be the key to
understanding why you're having such premonitions

Josephine Stiles

Well go on

Int: Angelo begins to recall his dreams.

Angelo Stiles

Well at first there were only clouds of opaque obscurity but
then I began to see beyond them as their veils of light
revealed pillars standing upright formed only of denser matter
reaching up and beyond the level of my eyes, each one of us
within the grasp of the other only shadowed by the clouded
veil that stood as an open archway and as some kind of
partition separating one archway from the other in its' purity
is pure light that can only portray us as we once were, shades
within its' midst, the veil is all but a shadow to something
much more greater, it is the source and sustaining light that
is everything even cast in us as its' sentient's, within this
it serves as an emittance of light from within the pillars
that stand to shade us with only glimpses of each other to
know what the greatest veil shades us within and from

Mercidiah

Is that everything Angelo, think about it for a
moment, is that everything that you've seen?

Angelo Stiles

No not exactly, beneath the veils of light, there were
the stars, each one there below to serve as answers,
some more knowing than the others, also emitting their
energy, just to look and to linger upon them is enough
to know all, as they too are seated beneath and around
the pillars of light that shade us from the greater
veil, in my dream I can fly to the furthest star and see
nothing more behind me except the sky below me which
is all but an infinite sea ablaze, then I wake up

Mercidiah

Light and pillars, suggest some sort of place, which may be
heaven, the greater light could be God, but I'm not so sure
why there's nothing after he flies further away, something else
is out there, Angelo what did you see in the blazing sky?

Angelo Stiles

I'm not sure what you want to know, its' just
spaces that I occupy, I'm mostly drawn to the
darker matter, coz its' denser I guess

Mercidiah

He must be the light itself, I believe he can only penetrate
through dark matter or denser forms of light allowing him
to see through too it, Angelo what did you see in the sea?

Angelo Stiles

I saw an angel flying with wings of fire

Mercidiah

Did you recognise him?

Angelo Stiles

No but I know his name, because the skies knew it

Mercidiah

What was it?

Angelo Stiles

Stefan, his name is Stefan

Mercidiah

If Angelo has indeed witnessed his father albeit in his
dreams through some trials of satanic judgment, then this
revelation alone could and would be a blessing in disguise

Josephine Stiles

I don't understand, this is Stefan were talking about

Mercidiah

For what dreams tell us about judgments if not the eternal
judgment of all mankind, has in this instance already been
passed, Angelo is not of the new natural order as of things
as I first thought, I now believe that his spirit is old, very
old in fact from the days of the original order, probably even
before Satan himself was formed, and so on Earth that would
make Angelo in heaven a cleric or some sort of a secretary
or someone who interprets God's decree, only for Angelo now
in this embodiment, he sees and witnesses God's decree as
dreams and then interprets them, and so as Earth Mothers we
must work to ensure his safety and balanced state of mind

Josephine Stiles

All this stuff is so overwhelming, if Stefan were here, I
think it would all somehow make sense, and that everything
would just fall into place, I'm just having a hard time living
up to the reality of what we are truly doing and even saying,
I mean what does it all mean, where is it all going to end?

Mercidiah

I know it's' hard for you Josey, but don't blame
yourself, some things are written in the heaven's
long before they are played out on planet Earth

Josephine Stiles

I know, I know Merci but what about you and
Simeon, has he ever made contact since…

Mercidiah

No not really, but I feel it's' for the best, although like
you I feel his presence all the time, everyday in fact

Josephine Stiles

And your blessed son Haven, how on Earth
could you give him up so easily?

Mercidiah

Haven is an Angel now Josey, its' best that way,
for him to be with his true origins, in my heart
I know he's my beautiful little miracle, that now
resides in the sanctum sanctuary of heaven

Josephine Stiles

Oh! My God Mercy, but why, why so puritanical,
doesn't it strike a sorrowful chord in you?

Mercidiah

Yes! It does, but its' the right thing for him, its' better
that he serves in the sanctuary of God's commandments

Josephine Stiles
I see, but if Angelo were away from me for
just one instance, I would die

Mercidiah
Angelo is a good Earth Angel, but I think of you as being an
influential Earth Mother, anyway independence isn't such a bad
thing, this story of age old love is only really ever between
two people, God and his subjects, the most hailed as being
Satan, and in reflection this Armageddon is as eternal as the
love that God has for Satan, even though he would not bow down
in the face of God's creation, but only sought to defy and
influence it to his own end, and now for countless centuries
God has allowed this one Angel to corrupt all of humanity,
every heart and mind forever tempted and provoked in the
anticipation that God would one day do away with his creation,
his love of man and woman alike, but we overcame time and
time again continuing to impress upon God's good graces
overcoming every trial of our endeavor to find a ourselves
back to serve him faithfully, the trial of Stefan is the same,
the theory or idea that God would eventually one day end this
everlasting love to a close, even in time that is eternal,
so we must continue to live out our lives with this faith and
understanding, surely that must make some sense to you Josey?

Ext: **As Stefan moved at speed and will over the mountainous
regions, even the ground and rocky terrains below seem
to shake and tremble with the sound of gravity's anger
forever pulling and weighing at him to yield to the plains
beneath him, even the soiled Earth did give way and fall
into the cracks and craters of the now bellowing opening
ground, swallowing up bodies of the Earth, until ridge ways
burst open sending up sulphurous smoke into the air laden
with moltenous debris arising from its' summit, creating
luminous arcs and plumes of volcanic ash.**

**When Stefan neared the mountain top, even their roofs did give
way, spitting out molten lave into the skies above while sending
down rivers hot molten lava along the mountain face into various**

cracks and crevices, creating fiery rivulets down the regions of its' slopes, down into the soulless sea below.

This was to be the beginning of Stefan's trial as he heard a voice coming from deep within the well of the mountain.

Angel Of The Abyss

Even now as you arrive, your presence is known amongst the saint's and the prophets and the entire household of heaven to bear witness to your trial

Stefan Stiles

Who are you, what bewilderment is this?

Angel Of The Abyss

Who is a liar, but he who denies the truth

Stefan Stiles

I deny nothing, this is the past you speak of, reveal yourself to me, I command you too

Angel Of The Abyss

For many deceivers have gone out into the world who do not confess

Stefan Stiles

But why, why am I being judged, I have served have I not, I have sipped from the cup of iniquity and poured out its judgment, what wrath can be upon me now

Angel Of The Abyss

They shall no more offer their sacrifices after whom this shall be a statue forever for them to judge throughout their generation

Ext: Just then the mountain erupted with a violent and raging explosion, and Stefan was caught up unawares and swallowed by the sheer power of the force, then he suddenly fell spiraling downward into the belly of the mountain, fearing for his life and his vulnerability to the terrifying and eruptive elements below, even as the moltenous seas flooded onto the mountains core, covering Stefan from head to toe, into a caste of burning lava ridden with the sands and the debris of the soulless sea, which quickly began to solidify, as the seas hardened into a caste of rock around him, creating a shell of an imprisonment, and then again with the waters slowly rising and flooding over this caged angelic statue, with only the angel of the abyss as its' keeper.

Angel Of The Abyss

They sacrificed to demons not to God, but to god's they did not know, to new god's, new arrivals that your father did not fear, if Satan cast out Satan then he is divided against himself, how then will his kingdom stand

Ext: As the angel of the abyss spoke out of the murky depths to the entrapped angelic figure, now slowly drowning inside the well of the mountain, the souls of the sea began to emerge taking on the form of sand creatures hardened and deadened by the molten lava, now creating a mist of sulphurous gases, although small in stature there were many of them, too many to be controlled or defeated by an angel now imprisoned in a caste of rock and debris, they began by pulling Stefan down into the depths below as commanded by the angel of the abyss.

Angel Of The Abyss

Pull! Pull! Pull him down

Ext: Stefan now fell like a rock of Goliath into the sands of the seabed floor, now caught up and bounded by the reeds and weeds, being pulled even further and deeper beneath the seabed floor, until there was no longer any sign of him to be seen.

Angel Of The Abyss

Unless Satan takes advantage of us we are not ignorant of his devices.

Ext: As the angel of the abyss uttered these final words, Stefan's cage and caste was completely swallowed up, disappearing

below and beneath the dark engulfing murky watery sands, all was now but still, as if nothing had happened but for one momentary second three particles of light began rising up and filtering through the sand and the waters, rising higher and higher into the oblivious skies above, containing only the elemental remnants of Stefan's heart, mind and soul.

Int: **By now Josephine and Mercidiah are discussing at great length the meaning of Angelo's dream whilst attempting to interpretate its' significance, Angelo on the other hand is sitting upstairs outside on the roof having climbed out of his bedroom window, to be in a space where he can think, meditate and be at one with himself.**

Mercidiah

I sense a great amount of loss and sorrow in you but you shouldn't think or even feel that way Josephine, it has never been in the historical hierarchal sense of the order, that the father and the son should be in the same dwelling place or household, let alone even live together

Josephine Stiles

That's ridiculous, its' ludicrous that's what it is, I don't get it, Why! Why not, Why is it so bad, what's wrong with it, what's so wrong with being the ones we love

Mercidiah

Josephine please try to understand, the love you speak of comes from below, the truth is we have a duty and a relationship to serve our greatest humanity, Angels don't just live out simple and ordinary mundane lives', they are our highest endeavors' and our unknown incomprehensible achievements, they take upon themselves what we would not nor could not by any means achieve or withstand, going far beyond any call of love, it is through their being that we are at least granted the lives that we do live by and the love that we do cherish, is that not love in itself?

Josephine Stiles

Stop it mercy, just stop it, surely its' not what God would have wanted, I don't believe it, I cannot accept it, its' just not my idea' of heaven, I just don't think that we all go around this self perpetuating merry go round, walking in and out of each other's lives, making impressions and impacting on each other for no reason whatsoever

Mercidiah

This state of thinking and feeling is not good for you Josey, to think or act in this way is too primal

Josephine Stiles

No Merci, its' human and its' my right to be just that

Mercidiah

Think of Angelo, think of the future, soon his seal will be removed and history will come into play once again, and he will be required to play his part in it, as much as you are here to be an Earth mother

Josephine Stiles

History! Hierarchy!, Hierarchy! Heaven, that's one H! Too many in my book, Why! Why!, Why are we forever indebted to this study of stupidity of what has or hasn't already been written or happened yet, can't you see Merci, can't you see were just as important, and just as valuable as these ageing timeless deity's we give so much credit and attention too"

Mercidiah

Yes, yes we are

Josephine Stiles

Then help me to win him back Merci, help me to play a part in this so called history, surely there is something that you must know or something that we haven't thought of, something that we can do to…

Mercidiah

...Josephine, please you're pushing me and the boundaries a little too far, I don't think that you have grasped the true role of our sister, no! Motherhood, yes flesh and blood is what we are truly are but our knowledge the sheer history of all these women chosen both now and in the past to fulfill things that...things that if only you knew, do you really want all of this to change, is that what you want?

Josephine Stiles

I just want what every woman wants', what anyone would want, I want my love beside me, yes, and I want Angelo to grow into a wonderful person, and I want happiness, most of all I want true happiness, unhampered by world saving feats of madness, its' not my doing and it certainly isn't my war, but somehow I've lost everything because something or someone say's otherwise, well I also have a need, and if that's what you mean by things having to change, then yes, that's what I want

Mercidiah

Very well then, you can start by packing your things

Josephine Stiles

Why! Where are we going?

Mercidiah

We are going back home to America for a start, first stop my place and then I will take you to a place that was once a sacred and fertile ground, from there we will need Angelo's blessing to guide and help us undo all that has transpired and hopefully re-unite you with your destiny

Ext: When Josephine, Angelo and Mercidiah finally arrive back home in the U.S.A, once they settle down, Mercidiah begins by looking up some notes and detailed references, in connection with the birth of Stefan and the strange circumstances relating to the death of Selah his mother. Meanwhile Angelo, is exploring some of the mystical paintings, talisman's objects of alchemy, and unusual palmistry books relating to spiritualism that are used in the practices of none other than that of Mecidiah otherwise known in these parts

as Madam Madinique. Who is by now flicking her way through the pages of some kind of Astrological Almanac.

Mercidiah

It says in this, relating to the past based upon what we would seemingly try to project or base our future outcomes on, or to attempt to interpret our future predications on, can only occur whenever of wherever we allow the past to influence us

Josephine Stiles

What does that mean?

Mercidiah

I think by chance we relinquish control over it by our present or constant affect on each other, so what we must do is to allow for time both past and present to become a constant or eventual pattern until it defines itself with every other eventful moment, until it arrives at the point of time where there is an ultimate answer or ideal outcome

Josephine Stiles

But what is the ultimate answer, even if there is only one, how do we bring it into our present if Stefan is already in oblivion

Mercidiah

Well not exactly, he is any and everywhere all at once, so to speak, as an Angel is a being of an enlightening and profound nature, then we must believe and accept that as we examine these relative points it is as if this was the greater resolving solution, but before we can act or engage with a prediction, the presence in the force must grant us a sign or demonstrate some overwhelming force as a time to engage with him

Josephine Stiles

So we engage and make our efforts to use this force to influence Stefan, do you mean that we can change his ultimate course, even if he were destined for oblivion?

Mercidiah

Yes!

Josephine Stiles

So maybe we can re-trace Stefan's flight through
Angelo's visions to figure out his journey

Mercidiah

Yes' well maybe if we go to the burial ground of Stefan's
mother, this will present us with the opportunity to engage
with his passage before he passed over into oblivion

Josephine Stiles

But what if we cannot influence his path, what
force are we calling into question here?

Mercidiah

I had a feeling about that already, but clearly like you said
earlier what does history have to do it with it, especially
when there is nothing greater than the force of love

Josephine Stiles

Love!

Mercidiah

The questions surrounding this paradox is that when we
were created, even we as mortals were granted power over
the Angels, albeit but one did not bow down, so in truth
if we command any angel especially that of our beloved,
then he must obey, for they are naturally our sentients

Josephine Stiles

So to put it another way, If I were to command Stefan to come
forth out of oblivion, then he must serve my commandment

Mercidiah

Yes! Exactly even out of oblivion, I
couldn't have put it better myself

Ext: As Josephine and Mercidiah continue to talk, Angelo is sitting upstairs outside on top of the roof, seated in a crossed legged position with his face toward the sun now shining in the sky, his eyes are closed and his arms are outstretched and extended against the length of his width. The wind quietly sweeps against his face as he is now in trance and meditative state, internally flying within the regions of his own mind which is now completely open to all the elements beyond and the heaven's above, residing upon a plane which no creature had ever given witness too, fully capable flying and gliding and diving through the heights and through the depths of an inner and outer world to places of unimaginable colours, shapes and boundless beauty and wonder, beyond the eagles gaze, over mountains and even deeper and through to the depths of the seas, finding and knowing no barriers within places and spaces that he extend the wings of his mind into, for a moment Josephine call out to Angelo and disrupt his meditative state.

Josephine Stiles

Angelo, can you hear me, do you understand what's happening, what were planning to do, we need you to interact with us darling, it's important

Angelo Stiles

Nothing's wrong, I know what you want, I'm concentrating on meditating, I'll be down in a while

Mercidiah

Angelo! Please come down, you can continue your practice later, we need to talk with you now

Angelo Stiles

Ok! Ok! Just let me dream this last flight, give me five more minutes Ok! And then I'll be down soon Ok! I promise

Ext: For a second, in a transcendental flight of images and places in Angelo's mind seem to blur and darken, but not before he floats loftily against the edge of the stratosphere where the clouds are beneath him and it is there and then that he closes his eyes over the heaven's before him just as he re-aligns with his meditative state and opens then once again on the rooftop of Madam Madinique's house of clairvoyancy.

Angelo Stiles
I'm coming!

Ext: Once Angelo comes down from the rooftop of Madam Madinique's house of Palmistry, Tarot Readings and Clairvoyance, Josephine and Mercidiah, get ready to make their way with Angelo to the remote burial ground of Stefan's mother, Selah. For a second Angelo pauses and looks directly into his mothers eyes.

Josephine Stiles
Are you Ok?

Angelo Stiles
I'm fine

Josephine Stiles
Good

Ext: From there on, there was only silence in the car as they drove to a place some only refer to as God's Stone, and as they arrive, the evening sky falls over the resting ground casting only shadows in the moonlight, suddenly all around is still except for the intervals of birds chirping in their nesting places, and the odd intermittent busyness of rodents scouring around, foraging for food in the darkness.

Mercidiah searches among the headstone engravings, until she finds the name of Selah etched and carved deeply within a slightly overgrown tree, which is hides part of her grave.

For a moment Josephine and Angelo stare together as this solemn and unkept unattended milestone, which seemingly appears pitifully neglected and yet timeless, now teeming with the growth of plant life, decaying blossoms, weeds and wildflower. Josephine turns to Mercidiah, looking and feeling vulnerable, helpless, doubtful and even scared of what this may conceal.

Josephine Stiles

I don't know what to say, I mean how do we, how do I find the inner wisdom, the strength and the courage to change something that has already been so significantly statuesque, steeped and now buried in religion

Mercidiah

You don't need to change a thing, you need to add to its fulfillment, its' not about trying to change the past Josephine, its' about our influence on the present, the past had already done its' own doing to motivate and empower us so much so that something above needs and cries out for its' own fulfillment, as a woman in this spiritual world, we act upon our divine role, steeped in religion but not buried, don't try to think of its' structure, think only of it, as everything as a whole

Josephine Stiles

But I am thinking of it as a whole

Mercidiah

Then you must believe in your heart and mind that it is so, and by doing this you can release your greatest fears and accept your greatest desire

Josephine Stiles

My desire, suddenly I even feel fearful of my own desire

Mercidiah
Ultimately love is unconditional, so whatever we
yield to it, is enough to give us comfort and
carry us from one lifetime to the next

**Ext: Just then Angelo becomes excited and alert to something in
the atmosphere. He points outwardly to the night skies.**

Angelo Stiles
Look there!

Ext: But Josephine and Mercidiah see nothing above.

Mercidiah
I think it's' already begun Josey, now no buts, for I
do not speak of faith now, only out of truth, so speak
your truth to the heavens or do not speak anymore

**Ext: Suddenly three lights appear above them descending from the
night skies, dancing in air like fireflies, flickering like
star lights above their heads, until a shadowy embodiment
of a ghostly figure comes forth glowing in the darkness
that surrounds them, it was plain now for them all to see
that it was Stefan now in between two worlds of light and
darkness.**

Stefan Stiles
Yearning I have known, and for too long loneliness has kept
me company beside me instead of you, memories that once
burned and abandoned me now remind me of my feelings as
my heart has now travelled through the ages of time to find
its' rightful place, so speak no more for I have heard your
voice carried through to me on the winds of change, and the
wings of desire were chains at my gateway that did bind and
hide me in the shadows of oblivion, seek no more to find me
in other worlds, as I am here even attentative to you and my
son who has seen through to me and I did see you also as the

embers of hell fell all about me, I am even now prevailing
only to the justices of the light that shines within you

Ext: **And then in that moment he was gone, vanishing into the
vast distant realms of the stars but only for a second,
within which to give way to an event horizon that led to
an instant transformation and re-birth of his former self,
for now he was returning home and once again he was made
whole as angel descending from the heavens above as the
fire flight of desire was now complete.**

ANGEL BABIES

A WING & A PRAYER
THE EMANCIPATION OF ANGELO STILES

ime is neither here or there, it is a time in between time as it is the beginning and yet the end of time. This is a story of the Alpha and the Omega, the first and the last and yet as we enter into this revelation, we begin to witness the birth of the Angel Babies a time of heavenly conception when dying Angels gave birth to Angelic children who were born to represent the order of the new world. The names of these Angel Babies remained unknown but they carried the Seal of their fathers written on their foreheads, and in all it totalled one hundred and forty four thousand Angels and this is the story of one of them.

They say that the Angels dwell and reside just beyond the mid points of the firmament, and the unseen world between the Heavens and the Earth, they say there are Legends written and spoken off across the ages and many are called but few are chosen, and whilst my life is full and complete and yet there is little I have achieved or even cared to have challenged, and I do not claim to possess the key that could set mankind free or even set my life on a true course to fulfill my own or anyone else's destiny.

So seldom are the descendants of the ascended Angels mentioned, but here on Earth in my home and domain I can see many symbolic representations and manifestations of the very legacy to which I belong too, and bearing upon this land which has been fought over for many a legacy and legend, shall always remain present but forever untold, for our true story is only written in and upon the hearts of those who know us, but do not necessarily know our presence or our names but for the record you can call me Angelo.

157

After my Father returned from Oblivion, I felt that something had finished and I was now content with fact that his trial had come to a perfect conclusion even though perfection itself is questionable and somewhat incomplete, but still I could see myself and him in my dreams as we were forever destined to re-live each experience for the rest of our lives. Even as my life was still unfolding, almost like the steps of a ladder leading me through a narrative of my journey, which was already written and somewhat set in stone just as these monuments and statues overlooking the halls and archways of Churches and Monolithic places.

I was always aware that my Eternal Earth Mother knew far more than she would actually say or express, but sometimes she would look at me knowingly with a smile or a silent stare of assurance, something which always gave me confidence especially when I felt or had any doubts about my own life which was now hanging in the questionable balance.

The more I knew about love the less I wanted to learn about other things, I felt that other things were merely a distraction to what love could possibly truly mean, and every night I would dream of the world being united in this perfection of beauty, simply because deep down I felt my Mothers feelings and emotions influence me, and I knew that if my Father was ever put through any more acts of tribulation again that she would never be the same person whom we loved so much, and I have always thought that one day I too would also be called into the unknown chapters of my Father's legacy and face the challenges of Humanity and the nature of my very own being and character.

One day before I left home to embrace upon my own curious desires of love and life, my Mother entered into my room as if to say goodbye and reveal to me my destiny in simply saying to me that it is time and that I need not to worry about my calling, as she would be with me always wherever I wish to go and that her blessing was with me and my Father, and that sometimes to have one blessing is too much and yet to have two blessings is a miracle.

The Moments seem to pass quite quickly and I was left with the thought of how I might one day find a blessing of my own, to love and to cherish the way that I was, I could never explain my dreams to my parents as I could hardly make sense of them myself, in fact it felt as if I were in between dreams and reality and the only thing guiding me through it all was a voice in the wind and the wilderness of the World, the voice was comforting me as if it knew me from within, calling out to me Angelo! Through the open window and out through into the open door of the unsuspecting world outside that I wished to learn and know more about.

As I matured with every step and encounter of travelling through life and the learning of subjects that would give weight and gravity to my minds imagination, I sometimes forget that love was the path that I had first intended to take as the world at first was seemingly huge and influential in all its' complexities of life, and as an innocent witness of mankind I also forgot about the voice that once called out to me from within the dreams and the depths of own my heart.

My first experience of this world was love, albeit in an unconditional manner and from that did I take from my mother's love for me tenderness, and my second experience was life and how to challenge and embrace it, and it is this much that I have taken from my father, but one Angel alone cannot change a world which is now set by its' legacy of legends and forbearers, as there is nothing here that I wish to change.

It is almost the ways of mankind have been set down and carved out by these vacant statuesque monuments if only for me to now gaze, wonder, love and appreciate in all its' symbolic gesture, as I sense it's every presence in the calling of my reality, I am merely a shadow and a familiar stranger to the ways of humankind, that is until I felt or at least came to learn the nature of what I thought was a kindred presence, as another Angel unknown to my being, but before I bring you to the attention of this if by per chance happening, let me first give you an insight into my perception of the world.

Although some of us are called as guardians and protectors of the vast land held in our sights by the presence of the Sun and the Moon, there are evermore reasons not to be seen or heard and that is simply because humankind is constantly in a state of preparation for that which may only be obvious to a few, and that is we are at best already ready.

And so what do the inhabitants of this fragile and beautiful world do but insist and persist to make their world and their lives ever more harder and all the more complex by creating problem and tasks one after the other, and in my observations it is only this, that she is not really ready to see this world as it is, or merely as he has constructed it, perfect.

But there is always a but, if everything is perfect then why does there always seem to be something missing, something left undone in need of attention from this our complex lives, and all of this my friend is where I come in, for I do not bear witness or give account, nor do I protect or observe of my infinite time that I dwell here with you for.

I am simply a visionary, something that can clarify and add perception and give meaning, something that puts the miracle inside the dream about to be realized, I see and feel beyond the edge of all darkness and reasoning, illuminating beyond the shadows of doubt wherever they are cast.

Many Suns and Moons ago I sat in the religious temples and watched as the mortals of humankind among us were praying and worshipping to the eternity that bare and borne them, laying gifts and flowers at the feet of their deities, in the hope of a sign or a prayer or a blessing to befall upon them and in truth some were somewhat disheartening and discontenting, and in some way many were unfulfilled and some were even saddened and lowly of heart and spiritually in need of comfort and reassurance.

And although I could have intervened or influenced them at their altars, I did not, nor did I choose to ignore if only to take note and to remember, for I knew that one day these days were to be short lived, and endured no more, because in these temples and at these altars Men, Women, Children were changing, and being changed unconditionally for the better, for the future and for good.

Which brings me back to the point of that which I am concerned with and that is An Angel or thereabouts, until well that is, until I truly met one, you see although I do possess Angelic like qualities, I do not naturally come with all the brilliance, display and splendor of such mythical beings, but as a child I have learnt to fly with my mind and there is no place between the Heavens and the Earth that I have not visited or become a part off, except one place, a place of exceptional beauty, an inner sanctuary, a place where fairytales become reality, and a place where reality becomes no more, no more than just the dream which we have all dreamt since we were the Angel Babies.

And so here commences the union of the Heavens upon the Earth but unlike my father and our predecessors, I did not fall from grace into Love, No! it was more like a metamorphosis that I did not know I could become, but it was through a series of events that opened my eyes and my mind and my heart to endless possibilities, and the truth that eternal love is no more mortal than you or I, but a union and a marriage of a world within worlds and a galaxy beyond the stars as only a vibration shimmering more vast than seas below or the winds above, and yet to see it is to become blind, and yet to touch it is to lose ones senses, and yet to smell it is to fall asleep beneath its' aroma, but to taste it, is the nectar of the honey and the ambrosia of all the fruits that yield to the God's of contentment.

This place is not for the senses to fear but for the heart to yield and become one within its' inner world, this place I do not know but I have felt as much, in its' calling out in its' every whisper, passing me by at every shadow if only to glimpse it for a moment within the passages of time but my heart was to shallow and too closed to truly recognize, that in all the signs that were appearing and vanishing at will before I could be sure and certain that in each revelation, and in each daydreamt vision things were being revealed to me, if not surely, if not suddenly, then unknowingly so, I could not predict how or why.

That is until I began to meditate and allow my mind and thoughts to focus beneath this ordinary and tame existence that I was in subjection too, and that was in subjection to me, for I have heard many a mortal whisper, is this all there is, when things are not always permitted to transcend or prevail into this world or the next, Be patient she said, as she flew into the shadows of my mind while a naked infantile cherub appeared, disappeared and reappeared momentarily, when all I could do is sense briefly the calling which was becoming much more clear to me, closer and closer until my mind could endure no more and I began to tire until finally I slept.

Then the night fell over me with the Sun rising upon the horizon within my mind's eye and there she was beneath the clouds like a bird of beauty suspended under the protection of the Sun disguised by its' rays, and for a moment I held still for I could not move, as if pinned to the place where I lay resting, and then as the clouds covered the Sun's rays, momentarily I moved and she was gone, if only for me to open my eyes awake and find that I had dreamt the entire thing in my sleep, to awaken to find my solitude and my thoughts beside me.

I have not known loss or sorrow, I have not felt sadness or misery but today on this day it was as if they had found me, I say this simply because before this brief encounter in my dreams I could comprehend and understand even the most complex and unexplainable things that I have ever come across, I could analyze, deconstruct and simplify the intricate and infinite detail of puzzles that challenge the minds intelligence and perception, my way of life was to undo all that was done and to know it as nothing more that as it is, but how do you explain something that may not have been, how do you challenge something which is fleeting and in perpetual motion, constantly changing, how can you grasp something when you cannot hold it in your hands, suddenly I felt my Genius break, slipping into the unknown and that what I could once easily fathom, was by now nothing more other than a ghost to me, a phantom of images, energy of sounds, challenging my every move, my every thought, even anticipating my every action, and who was I to say if this illusion of mirages could consist of something evident and of some real tangibility, how was I to know if what I thought I knew actually knew me, far more than I knew myself.

When I was a child I use to imagine distant and faraway places, places filled with awe and wonder, I could project and propel my minds imagination into alternate dimensions and then follow the path of my minds imagination to new and majestic places and I could play amongst the stars and the spirituals even of the surrealist imaginings of my inner sanctuary, and in each world my steps would follow each path as it unfolded before me, and I was always safe and sound, this is who I am and this is what I was, could it be that it was all coming back to me now, because now this other feeling is persistent and transient, and prevailing, this muse is secretive and elusive, a missing and mystical omnipresent.

Angelo! she whispers, and I know she knows me by name, and my mind, body and soul are obedient and responsive, but this feeling is a tug of war and I am off balance and insecure, I am curious and conscientious, I am bare and open wide, possessed by her aloof will, her presence disturbing and breaking into and beneath my will and rock of foundation, unearthing my confidence, as I am called into question, my wall is shattering piece by piece, and I am defenseless to this thing which can cause change and upheaval from the stars in the Heavens from the heart of the Virtuous soul, ANGELO! And I know she knows me.

And at her humbling mercy once again a sudden flash of the naked cherub child running and laughing playfully in and amongst the mirage of my mind, vanishing instantly with the echo of laughter now left lingering in the air that surrounds me, Wait! Wait! I call out but its' too late and yet too soon for the childlike cherub to hear me, can you see me, she questions me from above the heights and the depths of my sanity, yes I reply, I can see you, where are you now, I inquire to ask, but there is nothing, no reply, no answer only the sound of my own inner voice, what is your name, who are you I ask, once again, be quiet and speak with your heart, appears the childlike cherub in and amongst the midst of resolution, do not speak or utter in the silences, speaks the cherub as the mist disappears and vanishes hiding the cherub from my sight once again, close your eyes Angelo and see, I close my eyes and there standing in front of me is an Angelic like woman, fair and beautiful, draped in a bare garment, revealing only her nakedness in its' plain form, with bare feet and arms resting by her side, her hair flowed from her crown and fell onto her shoulders, and although it seemingly appeared that we could see each others' inner senses as length, I soon realized that she had no eyes, with which to see me with.

Who are you, where did you come from, Angelo, please speak softly, do not question the existence, but I am confused, confounded, please give me some understanding, or at least a little bit of enlightenment, the human in you is the analytical mind of slavery and persistent resistance, you have been here to long and a slave to humanity, when are you going to break free, break free, a slave to humanity but that's ridiculous, I serve a greater good, the same source and power that you represent, truly tell me how do you know me, what is this concern with me, yes it is true, we are one, together but not as you know or see it, the things influencing you now are no more, remnants of the past, that imprison you, so you've come to free me is that it, but I am already free, there is nothing wrong here, that may be true but look at me, look deeply and transcend my barrier, as you have transcended all the Earthly matters before you, but my eyes are closed and yet all I see is you, what do you expect me to see or find, your beauty, your form, your grace, your purity, your blindness! Try and touch me with your mind and then try and see the world as it is, as it was, and then I will give an answer to you.

Just then I tried to do as she told me and I couldn't, in fact I became frozen, I couldn't move my head, or my arms, or my feet, I couldn't even speak, there was I standing in the presence of an Angel illuminating all light from her breath upon me, and here was I frozen still in complete darkness, and the more I tried to struggle or wriggle to break free, the more I could not, it took me several challenges before I submitted and yielded in defeat and as I became still, calm, obedient and peaceful, something strangely familiar happened, I could hear an inner voice yielding, saying Ok! I submit,

I give in, now free me, but emotionally, spiritually I was held in suspense, bound by my own reasoning, and again I became still and frozen, and then still and calm, and once again I heard this inner voice which I now recognized to be my own voice trying to communicate through the struggle, the thoughts in my mind, but disconnected from the will to use my mouth, to speak formally.

I understand I said, do you she replied, yes but its' tricky, kind of hard to handle, is this really me, is this what you mean, yes! But this is only the beginning; there is more, much more to it than just speaking with the purity of heart, try to touch me with the same calm emotion that you have now reawaken with me, once again I fought to break from my frozen invisible state of in action, but the more I thought to gain motive and control over my own influence, the more I was held in suspense until eventually my heart began to slowdown from its' intense struggle, touch you I said, but how, where, why, I cannot move, touch me Angelo with your desire.

Suddenly I could feel the warmth of my heart surrounding my inner senses with an overwhelming feeling, something that felt like butterflies in the stomach, or at least an heightened awareness washed over me, blossoming like the scent of flowers in spring, suddenly I began to see and acknowledge what I could feel appearing in my mind's eye, like a past reawakened in me, from the past or the present, or was I witnessing the future, I did not know and for a while it did not matter but I knew it as more than just memories, it was real.

Can you see me now said my Angel, I can see a dream I replied, am I just a dream to you Angelo, well no but wait a minute this is you, I mean this vision, you mean all of this is actually you, there is so much more to me than just the scent of flowering fields or the elation of butterflies and memories, but yes this is me she said.

Wow! I mean, whoa, hold on, No! Angelo you must forget this humanistic questioning, but I just, No! look at your hands, and as she spoke I looked at my hands and noticed that they were beginning to darken and blacken, as if I were becoming infected by some unknown poison, once again I panicked and tried to struggle, but I could not move, what's wrong, what's happening to me, please! My hands, my feet, my head, my body, you are releasing your former self, you are becoming a whole again, you are evolving out of decay, Decay! No! please don't do this, and then I heard my mind screaming out in what felt and resounded like a thousand screams from within my soul, one word, one name, and it was hers my Angel, ANGELINA!.

I thought you had forgotten she said, I'm sorry I said, please Angelina, despair, hope, hurt, pain, you must forget, you must release yourself, you must not cling to these emotions anymore, I thought you were lost, I was, No! It was I who was lost to you, I also had to evolve, nurture change, develop and grow, and when you were taken away from me and given unto the world through your mother, I remember something I said, but, No butt's! In time you can reveal all and everything to me through your will and not your words.

Just then I felt like I and everything else had sprang to life, I felt relieved, reborn, released and strengthened, invigorated, confident and lively, my mind became clear with a clarity, I was alert, awake and free to move, my body felt renewed and the darkened poison seeping through my veins and shedded skin was gone, disappearing, leaving me feeling whole and cleansed, and then I felt her hand upon mine, as she reached to hold me, but as much as I tried, I could not see beyond her face, a face that glowed with the light of grace and beauty, illuminating with energy, fixating my hypnotic gaze steadily in my mind, reading and piercing my every will and action of thought, knowing me internally, its' my eyes that you miss isn't it she said, Yes!, what else do you miss about me Angelo, I couldn't think to answer but then a thought occurred to me, its' because of me isn't it, you forfeited your sight to be with me didn't you, I did Angelo, I did but why, why give up your sight to be with me and to not see the world in all its' wonder and fragility, because this is not the world that I want to see she said, but you cannot even see me can you I replied, I can, how, how is that even possible, everything is possible if you believe it, even in losing your sight everything is possible.

But I want you to see me, I want to look at you looking at me, I want you to see what I have seen, I want you to witness everything, do you, yes I do, don't you want to see me, I do, then open your eyes, I cannot only you can open them, Me! How, pray tell me how and I will do it, you must promise me she said, promise you, promise you what, that you will show me eternity, eternity! But how, how can anyone see eternity, Angelo! have I not already shown eternity to you, just then everything fell silent and once again I could not think or even feel the emotion to think, I was dumbfounded and speechless, this, this is eternity, is this what you mean, that I should become blind for you to see, No! This is not so, but you must do something, what make a promise, to do what, to perform a selfless act, No! You must make an unselfish act, you must bring about an unconditional action, but that's what I've been doing my whole life, No! Angelo you've done nothing, how can you say that, you've never seen, just then I hesitated and realized my disposition…, please I'm sorry, maybe you have noticed that I find it hard to grasp what is happening to me, to us, tell me what must I do, I have already told you, yes but show me.

Suddenly I thought symbolically of flowers growing out of a harsh and barren crack in the ground, flowering up and then springing forth, but if faded away too quickly, but as it faded, it gave way to droplets of water, rain now falling upon the wasteland and withering flower and all around about us, but this too also faded, but then it gave way to colors' dancing in the puddles of water forming like oil paintings, rainbows, but this also faded, did you see I said, did you see that, I did, show me more she said, suddenly my heart was filled with joy, take my hand Angelina, and then as she took my hand, and we connected our fingers and thumbs intertwined to form a heart like shape and as we did this, two doves unfolded their wings and took to the skies, eventually they lit up the heavens which in turn lit up the horizon, and in the distant their silhouettes could be seen on the horizon, that's us I said, that's how I see us, is that enough, don't stop she replied, so we flew on and on upon the shaped emblem of our coupled hands which stood like statues carved out of stone depicting our heavenly bodies as two statuesque pillars joined throughout eternity, suddenly I grew cold, wait! She said, do it now, but I do not have a wing or prayer I said.

I shall be your wing and your prayer, do it now or awaken no more, so I thought and I wished, I wished with all my heart that Angelina could see the world or at least eternity, I felt inadequate, and it seemed naive and silly but I still prayed that even if I thought it possible then it could or should be so and that it was so, and in a way that is what I had wanted to see, I wanted you to see it, suddenly the doves returned and flew through our coupled hands, and then the rains fell casting rainbows overhead and then the flowers reappeared and I felt the wind rising beneath our feet as we were lifted up more and more and the skies broke over our heads giving way to shining rays all about us, open your eyes, and she did, Angelina's eyes began to open and she gazed into mine, and as we looked at each other and around and about us, in front and beyond ourselves, I saw the statues hollow and carved out of stone where we were once standing in what seemed like an eternity.

That is who we were she said, now we can both see, but there is one more thing that I must do for you, what is it must I let go of you, No! You must not, but I must let go of you she said, why! I don't understand you can see now surely this is what you wanted, but you do not have a wing or a prayer Angelo, but I have you. Then kiss me she said, and so as we embraced, we became locked in an embraceable kiss and I felt free and empowered with an immediate inner sense, overwhelming me with joy, and as we did, so my wings did give way to me and begin to appear as she had shouldered me to the point where I could now master myself independently, this is the reason why I came into existence, she said, your name was written upon my heart and once again I have released you except this time we are together.

And so you see they say that the Angels dwell and reside just beyond the mid points of the firmament and the unseen world between the Heavens and the Earth, And they say there are Legends written and spoken off across the ages and many are called but few are chosen and whilst my life is full and complete and yet there is little I have achieved or even cared to have challenged and I do not claim to possess the key that could set mankind free or even set my life on a true course to fulfill my own or anyone else's destiny but this dream, this dream is the dream of the Angel Babies.

"AND I SAW ANOTHER ANGEL FLY IN THE MIDST OF HEAVEN, HAVING THE EVERLASTING GOSPEL TO PREACH UNTO THEM THAT DWELL ON THE EARTH, AND TO EVERY NATION, AND KINDRED, AND TONGUE, AND PEOPLE, SAYING WITH A LOUD VOICE, FEAR GOD, AND GIVE GLORY TO HIM; FOR THE HOUR OF HIS JUDGMENT IS COME: AND WORSHIP HIM THAT MADE HEAVEN, AND EARTH, AND THE SEA, AND THE FOUNTAINS OF WATERS."

REVELATION XIV. 6, 7.

ANGEL BABIES

THE OTHER PLACE

When we entered the other place nothing could be more far removed, and yet familiar than the presence of love in awe and fulfillment, other than something that someone can only truly possess both in youth and childhood, and for a long, long time I forgot where I was going or indeed where I had come from, although I felt assured that these ideas' of questioning were no longer relevant to this new deliverance of expectation, and that I was by now beginning to realize without motive, was becoming more and more captivating the more I began to explore.

This is where you were conceived said my Angel to me, in this place where the waters of life never cease to end, no one can say for certain where it truly begins or where it truly ends but the only truth is that everything must return to where it had come from, even time itself cannot be considered an influential presence in this the other place.

As my Angel transcended, my thoughts and took hold and shape inside of my own mind, body and soul, I knew that I was being reborn and formed and tutored in my own being, although my former self was also transforming into something with which my immediate memory could not fathom, as I had already forgotten my true nature identity and ability to be something other than just human, a mortal being albeit so of genius with great insight if only into the material sense of being, and yet now my senses had truly re-awakened, and everything was different and yet nothing had seemed to change.

They say a drowning man sees the images of his life flash intermittently in front of his eyes like random pictures as he slowly loses consciousness, but here was I swimming in the waters of life watching my previous lives unfold at will and then vanish right before my very eyes like ghosts amongst shadows of the past which were now leaving me indefinitely and for good, with no regret or regard for what I was able to be or about to become.

Even as the clouds stood like pillars of monuments, towers that had no fixtures and archways that arcs across the sky with no grounding, sunlight broke through and into every crack opening, and every corner that could give way to shade, the motion was seemingly seem less and yet everything changed on this awesome horizon the very moment and second that I felt or thought to change my own mind.

We did not tire nor feel tired, nor could we stop or rest, as we were held in the eternity of something living, something breathing, something erupting and something evolving constantly at will. Paradise was indeed compelling, as this place could not be dreamt or realized by the greatest of imaginations or inventiveness nor could it be navigated upon to pursue a course through to our own destiny.

You are at one with me now spoke my Angel, and your eyes and your vision and your thoughts and your desires are now upon this horizon of eventuality and happening, everything must merge into one and support itself by reason of definition and sub-conscious collectiveness, we no longer have or possess reason or have the conviction or contain the knowledge of our own selves, even as embodiments that are held as souls and as souls that are inherited by spirits, we are no more flesh and blood than the very waters that give us life.

It was once said that to enter the kingdom of heaven, that we must first become like children, and now even in this moment I no longer felt the need of things that I would put in accordance with the world at large, it was all but a stream flowing eternally and yet it was even said, that the kingdom of heaven could be found in a grain of sand and yet we seek in it to contain it, but we have never found it in ourselves to walk along a sea swept sandy beach thinking and feeling that this heaven could be forming its' foundation beneath our feet, as no one could see that they were indeed already within this place.

You see the other place is relative to this time and this place and this existence, the other place is debated by society at large and analyzed by statisticians, bureaucrats and executives within institutions to invent and invest within its' vested interest, the other place has been carved up and served up by servants of civil propaganda in the name of Marxism, socialism, communism and democracy, the other place consists of commerce, economics, capitalism and vast ideologies, in that the other place is transiently being made ready and prepared for said my Angel even before this place is truly extinct, you must remain conscious, be vigilant be prepared for the other place.

The other place is realism withstanding reality, the fact that reality remains elusive and an unknown quantity in our hearts and minds, in our spirits and souls, the other place is what you want and expect it to be in spite of our individual efforts to remain independent, the other place can only come into effect through universal collective consciousness, upon the lateral lines where we all sub-consciously agree, the other place is considered an improvement upon a modern and more majestic place, the other place is evidently now but not now evidently sown, make preparations said my Angel, create some positive roads and avenues to the other place, grow with potential, realize your dreams, think of this race, these people and these places, consider them and then re-consider them in the other place again.

Even in this moment as if I had became nothing, an upsurge of energy still moved within me, on an upward, down and inward, I felt contained within the elements that some may attribute to the universe or stardust, absorbing great weights and distinguishing even between greater goodness.

The other place is as practical as it is adaptable as this the present place, potentially setting no boundaries or margins between the far left or the extreme right, the other place is as mythical as it spiritual, and as historical as even becoming eventful as it is unimaginable, the other place is what fiction is to reality and what reality is to experience and what experience is to knowledge and what knowledge is to truth, as truth is tantamount as being proportionate and of paramount importance and in accordance to this and the other place.

I felt death overshadow me, I felt life empower me, I felt love lifting me, I felt time question me, I felt truth examine me and yet nothing remained in me even as the child inside me was no more than the cherub in my dreams absorbing any childlike qualities that my soul ever possessed. The other place has fundamental origins within the four seasonal elements and it is unique as the heightened awareness of the six senses, the other place is constant and consistent with and without weight, length, depth and gravity, the other place is a projected future and the future present, the other place creates, grows, sustains and develops as in any other place with dew drops, rainfall, sunrise, and moon fall at the whisper of a heartbeat.

The other place is to believe, to follow, to change and to challenge perception of the matter and to find the ideas or the relative ideology to the questions and the answers that govern human nature, until it matters no more than the human race and the evolving states of the human being, both now in this immediate tense and also in the continued existence of the human presence upon this, that and even upon the face of the other place, as this place may reside within you, even whilst you may even reside in the other place, or until the voice of an Angel lingers in your heart and mind saying is it me that knows heaven or is it heaven that knows me.

ANGEL BABIES
PABLO THE IMMORTAL ONE

PABLO ESTABLO ESTEBHAN AUGUSTUS DIABLO

Once Upon time in the abode of the heavens lived an Angel known only as Pablo Establo Estebhan Augustus Diablo or simply Pablo the Immortal One, and as it was prophesied that he should be the keeper of the seal of the unwritten laws and serves as a witness of the probable outcome and determinate fate of mankind and humanity between the heavens and the earth and all the realms and dominions in the life thereafter.

Imagine what it is to live in a world with no need of sleep or slumber and yet imagine what it is to dream a dream in a world never to awaken beyond the realms of spirit and spirituality, this is the way and the path and the doctrine of the immortal ones, spiritual walkers from one world to the next, the eternal watchers of infinite space and time, the finite observers of dreams within a divine and ethereal existence.

The story of our Immortal or should I say journey begins with a simple goodbye or departure from this our sanctuary and our eternal abode amongst the presence of the chosen to yield, love, protect, embrace and restore to its rightful and former place, ever since the very beginning of our legacy was revealed to mankind and humanity. For when Pablo was given over and sacrificed himself to the realms of Papiosa and the soul cages, no one amongst the Immortals or the abode of the Angels could have predicted or could have given a witnessed account, of what could or would indeed transpire or indeed take place in such a place as where many an Angel would indeed fear to tread.

And so willingly and willfully the Immortal soul of Pablo is guided if not transported into a place which bears no proper name or has any true bearing or reference point that he could navigate himself across the stars homeward bound, for the soul cages are as much an inner sanctum of nothing inasmuch one may reflect upon himself, until all that he or she truly is, surely becomes completely unknown.

And this idea of thought is complete and true if it were not only completely applicable to the world of mere mortal man and women, conceived of flesh and blood, something of which the Immortal one is not, and so why when it was not fully and completely realized by Papiosa that Pablo could not become or be a subject or something seduced or even reduced to something that one would regard as being in an unfathomable state of nothingness if only for Papiosa to then manipulate to his own end.

Then consider this, for it is Papiosa's purpose to reincarnate himself again and again, gaining more and more influence, power and knowledge over everything else by manipulating and taking from it the precious possession of any and every ethereal soul however pure and potent and defenseless, until he himself could consider himself amongst the greatest of all deities however ill-conceived.

Now that the soul is still, the spirit begins to stir for even though the soul and the spirit are inseparable, they both two dwell upon separate plains that make them a whole, this is also true for mankind and humanity but again let me remind you that it is not so for an Immortal Angel such as Pablo Establo Augustus Estebhan Diablo, for if there were no quality of uniformed unity and unification in both complete wholeness within the very core of an Immortal Angel, then he could not nor would not possess the power over integrity, innocence and servitude toward humanity and mankind if only to possess this power to save a soul from damnation or destruction.

Now that we have been made aware of Papiosa's meddlesome and rebellious intentions and independent nature to be and to become all things to all mankind, all but once never challenged, questioned, judged or called into account and yet in leaving Papiosa to his own manifesting divisiveness, it is as if it were somewhat permitted or allowed, or acceptable for him to continue by all of those who knew of him and the soul cages however remotely connected to this somewhat unconcerned adversary of heaven and advocate of something which was by now seemingly somewhat sinister, that was by now frequently coming and going between one realm and the next to do as he pleased.

Now no one knows how long Pablo the Immortal one slept or remained awake in the soul cages or how many times Papiosa would attempt to deceive or defy the Immortal One, but what we do know about this trial and ordeal is that Selah the beloved of Hark had already transcended the soul cages and that their heir and son Stefan had returned from Oblivion guided by Angelo and that Angelo was purified and reconciled back to the heavenly and holy place that is the abode of all sentient Angels, and so now we shall go beyond the soul cages to truly examine and look at the world itself, if only to peer into and understand the inner sanctum of Pablo the Immortal One and the challenges set by Papiosa to confront humanity and mankind.

Imagine having entered into heaven or hell by means of international transport unknowingly, becoming an unconditional subject to laws of the universe, No! Well maybe you have but you were not aware of the transition, this story albeit one of incomprehension is about a journey we all take every day, unknowingly but willingly without question or even answers and yet in every motion and moment we encounter an unquestioned but captured thought or image of the realms constantly at struggle with itself albeit we may be travelling through or in the realms of what some might regard as the six depths of hell or the seven highs of heaven.

Ext: Imagine standing on the earth looking up to heaven at the clouds and the stars, almost beginning to wonder if there is something out there beyond our understanding, wishing or hoping that somewhere in this vast universe, that there is the mere possible chance, that even with this simplistic childlike view that we all possesses in the way that we see or even begin to look at our world, or to guess beyond the naked eye of truth, that maybe this view of heaven, is only but a glimpse upon the surface of what may truly be laying beneath the surface, never really knowing the

clarity or true perception needed to penetrate beneath its veil, is simply just to share and to feel and to accept this notion from time to time.

Ext: The Arrivals

Airline Pilot
Could the passengers of flight 745k please fasten their seat belts as we are fast approaching our destination and will be landing very shortly

Train Driver
This train terminates at the next alighting point, could passengers please ensure that they follow the guide provided

Ship Captain
This is the captain of your ship speaking, we hope that you have had a satisfactory and pleasant journey, we shall be dropping anchor very shortly, and so could passengers please allow yourselves some time before leaving this vessel

Ext: The People

Matthew
Martha dear, you can thank Jesus if there's no need to say goodbye

Martha
What do you mean by that Matthew?

Matthew
Well I haven't been totally honest about everything in our relationship dear, and I also know that to enter into the kingdom of heaven, well, well you have to be born again, its' quite alarming, even frightening Martha dear

Martha
That's Ok Matthew you were christened as a child and baptized, surely after all those years of backsliding you can be honest with yourself now?

Matthew

No Martha that's not what I mean, what I'm trying to say
is that there was someone else, you know an affair

Martha

Another women, well Matthew, I'm surprised at you, after
all those years we've been together, you choose this moment
to tell me you've been with another women, its' quite
funny really I suppose, I should come clean myself to
tell you the truth dear, in our thirty years of marriage,
there's been several other men, well affairs if you like,
but I would always come home back to you, you're the one
for me my dear darling Matthew, you're the one I love

**Ext: Move along, a voice shouts from the people alighting and
gathering, some still departing from the newly arrived
vessels.**

Man One

I knew it, I knew it all along, is simply confirms
everything I ever thought, what can I say, it confuses
me deeply, it saddens my heart, I use to say to myself,
you're not going to make it but we did didn't we, I
mean we have, haven't we, we have, haven't we

Man Two

Oh its' far too late for idle chatter, if I answered you,
if you answered me, if anyone answered anyone, would that
be enough to see us through, I mean no sense of purpose,
no direction, I mean where are we going, where's everyone
coming from, I can't believe it, I just can't believe
it, does that make me a non-believer, well does it?

Man One

If you don't move along, you might not make it

Man Two

I don't see it like that

Man One

No! Well how do you see it exactly?

Man Two

Well its' all in someone else's time,
but it's my time now somehow

Man One

I was thinking maybe I won't make it I use to
say to myself I just can't take it anymore,
no sense of purpose, and no direction

Man Two

No direction, no direction, what do you mean, look you've made
it, look around, look at all these people, all these faces,
all these souls, are they all lost, are they, what are they
looking for, what are they doing here, what are we doing here,
who's right anyway, you! Me agreed, as long as we need or
have a sense of purpose, some kind of direction, as long as…

Ext: He pauses

Preacher

As long as you have Jesus, Oh lord God! Jesus Christ,
help us, we beg for mercy and forgiveness in your name,
we are unworthy lord but we are repentant, we ask for
your blessing and your guidance in this our final hour
and to be brought back to your everlasting love

Man Two

Yes, something to believe in, I mean Jesus!
Jesus Christ your quite right

Preacher

My friends, you and you and all of you, when God equip
me, still the Devil tricked me and strip me, when I
was naked I was fully clothed, an Angel caught me
but then a demon bought me and so much is the value
of my soul, God was good enough to love and tame me,

but not enough to blame me because I sow the seed of
love, we must sow the seed of love, to be blameless

Man One

Oh! I see

Man Two

What do you see?

Man One

Don't you see, it simply confirms everything I thought,
what can I say, maybe were going to make it after all

Preacher

Only the innocent seem to need me, when the
guilty need me not, with only a miracle would they
believe me, but why tempt the lord thy God

Man Two

But if someone turns their back on you, where are you
going to go, what are you going to do, in your own
private hell is where you'll be, if someone is hurting
you, who are you going to tell your problems too?

Man One

Preacher, Preacher! I'm going to tell it to the preacher

Preacher

No! I am unworthy vessel, tell it to God,
and tell it to God in Jesus name

**Ext: People began flooding off the Trains, Airplanes and Ships
and began to gather in the one place, some in bewilderment
and amazement at the glorious sight that they had now
come to set their eyes upon, not one of them knowing who,
what, where, how why or if they are arisen or what has
befallen them to deliver them to this heavenly majestic
place, those who left the Airplanes have yet to realize
that this is a turning point an alighting point, and that
this landing strip was unlike any other, and those who**

had alighted from the Trains could clearly see not only
the infinite running of rail track for miles and miles, but
other vessels such as Ships, and those who departed from
the Ships arriving into the port, dropping anchor whilst
docking, realized that this is no ordinary port but the
greatest sight to behold since the eighth wonder of the
world, the shimmering, blues, turquoise waters glistening
around them like a paradise untouched by human hand.

A stranger appears among them, no more different than any other
person who had just arrived at this point in time, it is as
though he has been here all along, but where did he come from,
none the less he moves among then freely his name is Papiosa.

Papiosa

Hey there fella I recognize your face but
your name escapes me, tell what is it?

Al

I can't say I remember you from any place, but
Al's the name, and who might you be?

Papiosa

Pleasure to meet you Al, but you say you cannot
remember me from any place, well I suppose only
time can tell, well it's time for me to move on but
before I go you must take care of yourself Al

Al

He spoke to me as if he knew me, that's funny, is
that possible or just completely ridiculous

Ext: Just then another stranger appeared from nowhere and his
name is Pablo the Immortal.

Pablo the Immortal

Al you are happy, and my friend is very instinctive
around happy loving souls, and love will say we are
of one, one of a kind and love is never wrong

Al

But you also speak to me as if you knew me from deep
within, I can feel it, I can sense it something familiar
like a memory or a past life, but tell me my friend between
the sun and the moon, I wonder if its' true what can
happen in heaven can also happen in hell too, I mean do
you understand me what I am trying to say, it seems funny
I know but I can't help but somehow see it like that?

Pablo the Immortal

I am appeasing, and compromising with my own feelings
also Al, this is a place that we know very well and
my friend only came to you with the intentions of
desire, if not of the deepest darkest notions, if
only to understand the nature of your pain

Al

He did, yes he did, he wanted to understand the
nature of my pain, but why me, why here, why now?

Pablo the Immortal

Did he bring to life the thoughts inside your mind
making you realize that you were only now ready to
begin to comprehend that your spirit or soul could
become broken or weak in a moment, in a whisper?

Al

I'm not sure, what that means, is my spirit or soul to become
broken, but why, what have I done to receive such a fate?

Pablo the Immortal

You have done nothing, that no one else here has done,
please be strong Al and carry on through the fears
and see beyond these tears and emotions of doubt,
love will say were of one and love is never wrong

**Ext: A Child wanders among the crowd with awe and interest and
excitement but very much unaware of what his presence
there is going to have as an effect on the others.**

Child

God's guiding, I was speaking, I mean I was mumbling, meaningful and meaningless, but I don't understand, I was shaken through with fear a fear of being forsaken, but its' not the way I planned, it was different in my dreams, but I didn't plan it like this, its' not the way I planned it at all

Pablo the Immortal

Are you Ok Child, gather yourself, your mind and your thoughts, you are young and agile, you have much to see beyond this place, and yes God is guiding you, as he is guiding all of us

Child

Thank you, yes I am fine now, I know God's guiding, I was beaten, I was feeling chastised, even through pride and compassion, it was scary, and I am tired and weary now, but still I do not understand it, does anyone here understand it, do you understand?

Pablo the Immortal

No! I am afraid I do not understand as you do

Al

The Child, he speaks with meaning because he is innocent and caring, kind and sharing, God is guiding him, but it is not the way that he had seen it in a dream or planned it, come child take a closer look at my soul, try to understand the nature of my pain, for me it is also meaningful and meaningless, it is a struggle and a fight but I cannot let go, I too am shaken but not forsaken, and it is not the way any of us had planned it, but God is guiding us every step of the way, is that not true my friend?

Child

I guess you understand it

Pablo the Immortal

Continue to speak with meaning for God has guided you to us

Ext: The Vision, Each and every person looks on ahead as something begins to stir with their spirit on the horizon, bright shimmering lights appear in the distance, clouds open up in formations, seemingly to appear and disappear and reappear at will, as if something were erupting whilst moving through space and time and beyond, the skies began to darken on this new horizon while the bright lights began to become even more and more distant, as the gathering of the people were in subjection and very much unaware that they were in motion and moving ever more towards the vision.

Ext: A Rastafarian points in the direction of the light that is surrounded by darkness.

Rastafarian

There's a black sky with futuristic clouds, look there on the horizon, I can't close my eyes, were on a mission to die, its' a lie, everybody knows the reasons why, because were full of suspicion, those raised from the ashes have come back to haunt us, we shall all simply turn to dust, I call on Jah! To remove this vision and show me the way, this is a black future without a face

Martha

Matthew darling, I can't close my eyes

Preacher

I cannot close my eyes

Papiosa

I See nothing, nothing but fear, I close my eyes to it all

Pablo the Immortal

Child speak, speak with meaning, tell me what it means

Child

The word it is born, born of flesh and blood has now become heed, God will answer this you and me, no pain or suffering for tomorrows heart, our happiness will elevate and shine for us, and in our prayers where we

fought for our dreams, we will not fight for our dream
any longer, for God will answer this you and me

Al

The glory of God is upon us, manners maketh man, the
journey has begun, a man can conquer the mountains, and
sail upon the great oceans wide, but a man can conquer
nothing more, it is time, it is time to put away those
former things and to embrace and understand that a
man cannot serve two masters, I will not close my eyes
but remain wise as the journey has already begun

Ext: **The entirety of the gathering crowd were no longer stationed
at the arrival point as they were now moving through time,
although time was now no longer of any importance, the
vessels in which they had arrived in as transportation
to bring them to this new place, were no more, but they
now each and every one of them had become the vessel in
which they had become the one body they had become the
one purpose as one would come to terms with the body of
Christ.**

Rastafarian

It is as though an Angel were here, it is as though
time has deteriorated and the light of eternity now
shines for what was the dying and the weak, the
suffering and the meek are all gathering here

Papiosa

I know the shepherd is your guide, he put your
name in the book of life as you so believed
and his love for you will never die

Rastafarian

Rasta's destiny tells the whole story,
providing Jah is there, I will go there

Papiosa

The truth may hurt when often spoken of
in clouded judgment and fear

Rastafarian

There is much need for hope and glory, can't
you see Its' as though an Angel were here

Papiosa

An Angel, is it not the same as the lamb and lion standing
side by side, this hope and glory you proclaim, the spirit
of Jah, is that what you believe you are witness too

Rastafarian

The spirit of Jah

Papiosa

Or the presence of an Angel as you so put it

Rastafarian

Yes, now the proud and the bold, the bright and
the beautiful, the lion in his kingdom, over and
over again, I will call on Jah as my friend

Papiosa

A friend in need is a friend indeed, but why should you
walk with foolish pride, why should you seek that which
you cannot find, this is the world that has surely lived
and died, this is the world that once was open wide but
now nothing more, nothing less, but a friend you say, that
which you know not yet and so easily come to call friend

Rastafarian

My friend I am born of slavery, by birth and by trade
I am set free and yet I have not known freedom, still
I remain in captivity, still the chains are with
me, if there is one thing a slave would understand,
is the life and the ways of the son of man

Papiosa

You are strong and wise and keen

Rastafarian

And you my friend you are cunning and clever
and careless to assume that you know me

Papiosa

Cunning and clever maybe yes maybe be not, but
I think your judgment of me precedes you

Rastafarian

I do not judge you in order that I may be judge
not, careless words and yet it takes one to know
one and you are one that I know so well

Ext: Papiosa moves on but still remains an unnoticed presence among the people.

Man One

Well here we are sisters and brothers, here
we are in love with one another

Papiosa

Here we are burning in hell wanting much more, we fall,
we rise but have we forgotten what we were looking for

Man Two

Do you want to die, have we forgotten, have you forgotten
what you were looking for, there is still a heaven, and
there will always be love, yes here we are crucified, and yet
sanctified, reaching for heaven and knowing nothing more

Man One

A plea if you please, a cry for help if only heard, wanting
nothing more, needing nothing more, but no I do not want
to die, nobody here wants to die do they, I want, we all
want to see the highest high, I want to be in heaven, and
I still want to remain in love, don't you agree my friend

Man Two

Of course I agree

Preacher
We were chosen by the need for immortal love, through
hate and pain we were subjected, and now we are
subjects woven by the intricacies of emotions, if not
for the love of God we would not have existed

Man Two
I desire the truth when all else fails me, when all I hear
is the words of a liar, I desire the truth, when the fire is
coming clear to my soul, I desire the truth, when the wages
of sin give way to death, I desire the truth, if it is my
last request, when led to the slaughter, I do not want to die
without the truth, I too want to see the highest high, how
can I trust this justice if there is no truth by my side

Man One
Believe me, now believe this and open your eyes, for it is the
spirit of Angels that which is manifest and a manifestation of
the spirit is a must, this must be the corridors of justice

Papiosa
Who amongst you have prayed to God and received
empty hands, who amongst you, have tarried
and turned away from the savior of man"

**Ext: Suddenly amidst the confusion everyone stopped to look at
Papiosa.**

Rastafarian
Come quickly, we must walk towards the light

The Chosen Ones

**Ext: Suddenly All the Airplane Pilots, Train Drivers and Ships
Captains were taken by surprise, for it were not their
job or they're their duty, as seemingly authoritarians
to give counsel and commands to the multitudes, who were
now heading toward the light which shone in the distant
horizon, a mysterious sky was now alight with brilliant and
bright colors as if the sky were on fire, clouds dissolving**

and reforming at an instant, as the people who now stood shoulder to shoulder as they begun to receive divine messages from the chosen ones.

1st Airplane Pilot

Forgiveness of sins, we thank thee now, redemption begins, the light from heaven is on earth, it is the baptism of a birth born of fire, we are now the confessions of the past, we have paid the fee through repentance, and we are released from the word, as the words have been released from us

1st Train Driver

We have exalted our hearts; we are rejoiced not as earthly but as heavenly creatures, here in the place in the presence of grace, here within this peace and this presence of beauty, here in this love

1st Ship Captain

It is for you, for us to journey onwards, so I say to you as is said over and over again to the entire congregation, a soul makes a man, a spirit makes a ghost, but we will never be the same but be sure to know we will never be alone, too many souls have been here before, some have perished and died, so make your peace with God and make your peace with Christ

Old Man

In my heart I have tried to walk with pride but slowly it fades away, I was down and defeated my wounds were untreated, now for all of my sins, tell me once more how love has conquered war

1st Airplane Pilot

You are no more living for one more day but are forever held in an eternity

1st Train Driver

Innocence is a great attribution, and there is a great way to behold upon us, this great day, for great sorrows are redeemed and yes love has triumphed over war

1ˢᵗ Ship Captain

On this great day, this great feeling inside of my heart
and my mind and that which we all rejoice in, is now both
yours and mine knowing love ever more, knowing love has
conquered war, in your hearts and minds yes you have
walked with great strides of pride but no longer will
it fade away from you for now we have become the way

Matthew

Don't let me die here Martha not in the hereafter

1ˢᵗ Airplane Pilot

Make your peace with God, make your presence felt

Martha

Use words of expression Matthew, like a child, teach a lesson
for us all, with words from the heart, from within your soul

Papiosa

Love was a philosophy, love is oh so precious Matthew,
there are and there were prophets of great wisdom who spoke
of love, it was depicted as a reign of rainbows and what
religion would you choose above this love philosophy?

Matthew

Love is still a philosophy isn't it, and much more,
I mean we look to God for representation

Papiosa

Yes but look how they judge you by your religion,
what love are you giving and sharing, what
life have you been living Matthew?

Matthew

They do don't they, they judge me by my religion, do you
really think it so, I am judged by the thoughts I possess,
what about my love of life, who am I giving it too?

Papiosa

To whom are you referring, to whom do look to for
representation, that's who, and ask yourself of your
life, that's who, who before time named the garden
of Eden, who before time brought to life all the
seasons, who Matthew, tell me who, answer me?

Matthew

It is them, is it me, you called me by my name

Papiosa

Fear is a curious thing Matthew; it is you and them
amongst you, that I call by name, for they presume
themselves to be born of the righteous ones

Matthew

Lies, white lies, to hell with them, only time will prevail
the truth, I was looking to God for representation

Papiosa

But to whom do you look to?

Martha

Matthew he's trying to afflict you with guilt, you are not
at fault, he works to convict you, casting doubts and
suspicions about you, try not to fear it, you were baptized
with the holy spirit, you were christened as a child, you
must fend off his words, you must prove your worth Matthew

Matthew

Why am I being deceived?

Martha

Because we are the righteous ones, because we truly
believe Matthew, because we truly believe

Papiosa

Intelligence or plain commonsense, will
tell you which way to go Matthew

Matthew

Don't let me be denied Martha, don't let me be denied

Papiosa

Choose Matthew, choose or deny your life

Ext: Just then the chosen ones began to address for the last time the gathering mass of people now awaiting the true purpose of their destinies, the message was clear and concise and yet unfathomable by the conscious mind, a message not of fatality or finality but of a new beginning, the voices of the chosen ones echoed throughout the congregation as they began to speak.

1ˢᵗ Airplane Pilot

There are six depths of hell to the seven heights of heaven, the light of life which shines eternally in the distance between night and day is the way, we are now one body, and we must move, think and feel as one

1ˢᵗ Train Driver

There are seven heights of heaven to the six depths of hell, that which was the end is now the beginning, and that which was the beginning is now the end, let us begin by entering the light

1ˢᵗ Ship Captain

There are as many depths as there are as many heights, and so as we move as one in these realms, and we must remain, true to each other in one single thought

Papiosa

You may well say this is the final hour Matthew

1ˢᵗ Airplane Pilot

Put away the those former things that you have come to know before, understand that a man cannot serve two masters, the stranger amongst you will not enter beyond this realm

Papisoa

Come Matthew

Matthew

I never knew I could be taken to a place without love Martha

Martha

Don't listen to him Matthew, he only
comes to seek after your soul

1ˢᵗ Train Driver

Do not be possessed or found without
love Matthew and you Martha

Child

The light, keep focusing on the light, its' here, its'
within and around us, its' uplifting and inviting us

Pablo the Immortal

I sense its' presence, a beauty of
enlightenment, elegance and grace

Al

The black consumes the space and the night beyond, its' a
void, No! No! Wait its' formed of white starlight its' in
the air we breathe, its' crystal clear, its' remarkable

Rastafarian

Yellow sun shining down on me, deep blue green
as the sea, grey like rain clouds in between, the
mother earth now blessed red, gold and green

Child

It is the light of life, it's within and around
us, it has no meaning, no reason, no reason
for speaking, but I understand it

Pablo the Immortal

It is complete and unknown to me, unplanned and yet
a rainbow of flowers color and cover the land

Preacher

From the line of David down to Solomon, your majesty since
history, you present the future that none could see, the
people many in one set free, blessed with life, love and
liberty, may this be the beginning, or may this be the
one, two, three, four, five, six depths of hell that we have
transcended into a seventh heaven, who would have known or
thought that they were to be found in the same place, on
the same plain, all that which is the essence of life, look
around you, do you not remember it as it was, as it should
be from Genesis to Revelation and beyond, I knew my heart
and mind was on a journey but where too I did not know,
they held a promise for me, that my eyes could not see,
although I have read the good book with good intentions
and preached many sermons with breath, it seems that only
now it all becomes clear, and now I know this place so
well you too Al, and you too Matthew and my Rastafarian
friend, you too have understood the stories foretold in
ancient times, in history, it was a sign, but very much
unclear at least up until now, In this its' appointed time

Child

But one thing I still must ask you, is how have we come
to know and understand that this is a reality or a vision,
with no comparison to truth other than that, which we
know only of ourselves from that which we know not

Preacher

Listen child and listen well, I believe we are bound by
truth inescapable truth, the truth of God holds me and
you from deep within, with no boundary, except by faith

Matthew

Look there on the horizon, who is it in the distance

Al

It is the stranger, he appears to be descending, but to
where he goes or what lies before him I do not know

Pablo the Immortal

Descending, why does he have reason to descend now, unless he may know what is to become of us or indeed his own fate

Al

Maybe he has a reason to be or to become that which he already is, I am certain, but to each his own and every one of us has a destiny to attend too, and each one of us are intricately woven into each other's lives, look no more upon the past and rest assure, he goes to fulfill his own end

Pablo the Immortal

And the comfort of the light which guides us within this feeling, that which overwhelms us, does it fail to teach and reach him also, why does he not take part and find peace with those of us who Seek to have this understanding

Child

What he takes away with him we will never know, but the guiding light which is our comforter, it glows thereabouts with him, just not so brightly or intently, there where he descends knows him more than we do, but we must leave him be

Pablo the Immortal

No I cannot, I will not let him leave us answered, unknowingly, I feel his indifference, I cannot abide with you any longer, I wish to know more of him, I will follow after him there where he descends

Ext: As Pablo the Immortal one turns away for the others as he attempts to pursue Papiosa who has by now departed from his place in space and time, a place where many have now come into their own understanding, he feels a pull or pressure as he goes against the very sanctity of his own immortal soul, as he attempts to defy all reason of totality, with no real reason why he must now pursue a course in destiny to finally breach a promise and break with faith to reach the point of no return and find himself rapidly changing and hurtling at speed across time, as he transcends and begins to descend upon the lower depths.

Pablo the Immortal
Where am I Papiosa, answer me, and tell what has
become of you, as I have come back for you, please
speak with me, and tell me what I have done by
returning to this place, please speak with me?

Papiosa
Where are we, you might ask my friend, when none have sought
to change the course of all things just to speak with Papiosa,
no one with any knowledge of life and death has attempted
or sought to question Papiosa except Pablo the Immortal,
and now you wish to know answers to that which questions
the very spirit of souls itself, well my friend, your are
three hundred and sixty five thousand days away from the
point that you were before you realized the seventh high

Pablo the Immortal
What is the seventh high?

Papiosa
I am afraid there is no other explanation for it, I do
not know it by any other name other than the empyreans

Pablo the Immortal
Who are you Papiosa, what are you?

Papiosa
I am Papiosa, I am many, I am a spirit and a vessel of which
many souls have passed through, I dwell here between heaven
and earth and the sun and the moon, but who are you Pablo

Pablo the Immortal
I am Pablo the keeper of the unwritten laws

Papiosa
The unwritten laws, what does that mean?

Pablo The Immortal
The unwritten laws, are statues that are performed
and stand outside the natural laws of creation

Papiosa

But how is it even possible, if they remain hidden
or unwritten, outside the laws of creation?

Pablo The Immortal

Everything is possible within the laws of creation,
therefore if the unwritten laws can be achieved or made
acceptable in thy sight, by either faith through prayer
or healing through the purity of heart and a pure mind
of good intent, then these acts can be witnessed on
account but need not be written in order to be granted

Papiosa

Then what you mean is, an act is achieved or
made possible, by the means of a miracle

Pablo The Immortal

Yes! The miracle being the unwritten law, if achieved
or granted cannot be recorded inside the natural laws
of creation, and so therefore the fabric or the metal
of this miracle cannot be made proven or verified
without divine intervention or any other miraculous
event in whatever form or shape it may take, and it is
I who keep note of it, whenever it is performed, and so
hence forth I am the keeper of the unwritten laws

Papiosa

And you who choose to turn your back on your own destiny on
the kingdom of heaven, to ask me these foolish questions,
knowing that you may never see the light or its' new
becoming, Pablo, the Immortal who chooses to breach
promises, break chains and take chances to come here,
here where your soul hangs in the balance, you and your
inquisitive nature, were to be blessed with everlasting
life where there are many more realms and depths even
beyond this one, but what have you done, by coming here
this day in paradise, may change the whole course of
your existence and that pertaining of heaven itself

Pablo the Immortal

I don't understand, Papiosa it is only because of you why
I came back to this point in time, I see you are without
a world, without a place, without a time, I needed to
talk with you, to know more of you, to know myself

Papiosa

There are those who know of I and for that reason I am denied
a life of knowing anything more than the seventh high, I bid
you now farewell and say goodbye for without a world, without
a place, without time, you would surely die, how I long to say
come please stay, but my heart would say, for how long can I
be untrue to the spirit that speaks and breathes inside of
you, come Pablo, I will help you to make it back from whence
you came, there is much for me to do and your being here would
only disable me, you have already thrown time into chaos,
and confused my time, with your strong convictions but I am
Papiosa and I am thankful for your being Pablo the Immortal

Ext: **As Papiosa spoke to Pablo the Immortal, time had already
begun to allow, for Pablo to begin his ascension back
through the six depths and back towards the seven heights,
he felt himself becoming more and more distant from Papiosa,
tears began to fall from his eyes and sadness had filled
up inside of him, and so Papiosa extended his hand and
caught Pablo's tears and allowed them to rain over the
lower depths, as he went on to descend even further where
more people were due to alight. His execution, his good
judgment had not gone unnoticed as his own emotions had
revealed himself, as he too knew the love of which he felt
on his encounter with Pablo the Immortal.**

Ext: **Now no one knew how long the rain had fallen in the lower
depths or how long it would take before it would finally
fall upon the earth or indeed why Pablo the Immortal was
now deeply and sorrowfully saddened and troubled by what
he had come to bear witness to concerning the journey
through the soul cages, or the fate that had befallen
Papiosa who was now left to ponder and wonder the lower
realms unbeknown unto any other except his own, and so
began the story of the unwritten laws and the probable**

outcome of Pablo the Immortal. In and among the midst of the realms of a singularity, there spoke a voice as if that were enough to conjure up the tears and the swelling of a heart beating inside its' own bosom.

Pablo the Immortal

I find it hard to say to you that my love has spoken although
I know not what time or day it is but I wait patiently
for that moment for I cannot begin without you, I know
where you dwell within the loneliness but I say believe in
me for I believe in you, come and go with me and I will
show you what you have done for me this day in paradise,
for it is apparent that you do not see the importance
of your being, your eyes were not open, come and I will
open them for you, the sun, and the day beginning

Ext: He pauses.

Pablo the Immortal

The sun and you have guided the way for many a kindred
soul to enter the kingdom of heaven but you did not, nor
could not enter, come go with me for I no longer wish
for you to dwell in nothingness, to each existence there
is his own and to each star there is an eternity and
your have eternally held time so that many may pass by
you, when in truth you are a star and a heavenly place
awaits you in the new heavens if not destiny itself

Ext: As Papiosa followed the rain down into the lower depths until the Earth came closer and nearer orbiting its' heavenly body around the sun there began a transformation of the constellations which were grouped there, matter was now forming and taking shape but somewhere on the face of the earth an astronomer was taking note of these peculiar astrological influences.

Astronomer

That's' unusual, a Dog Star in that grouping of
constellations, it seems to be a highly irregular
pattern but I'm looking at it and boy yep!

That's magnificent, better call Dean, he'll
probably be looking at the same thing

Int: The Astronomer calls his friend.

Dean Cosgrove
Dean Cosgrove speaking

Astronomer
Hey Dean, its Neal, ya' know from Stargazers Observatory,
I've seen the craziest thing ever going on up there, you
won't believe it man, something awesome that appears to be
very similar to Sirius, ya' know the brightest star, but
I must say that there are some highly irregular patterns
forming, but get this, I got a night shot of it as well,
which I'm developing now, it's brilliant absolutely brilliant,
something to be marveled at, maybe they'll name it after me

Dean Cosgrove
When can I see it?

Astronomer
As soon as its' developed, I'll catch the next
train into the big city, I'll call you on my arrival
you can pick me up so we can figure out what's
happening on up there, this is my headliner

**Int: The Astronomer Neal puts down the phone and goes back to
his darkroom when he takes the photograph from a tray of
developing solution, he dry's off the print and puts it
into a folder, he then grabs his rucksack and heads out
the door towards the mainline station. Meanwhile a student
sits' in his study room comparing detailed notes and dates
in connection with a seminar he has to attend, while his
daughter a girl named Kemi is also playing outside when
she sees a bright shooting star soar across the sky.**

Kemi
Daddy! Daddy come quick, you won't believe what I
just seen, come quick now before you miss it

Kemi's Dad

Not now Kemi, I'm studying, I've got work to do

Kemi

No! Daddy quick or you'll miss it, its' a shooting
star, it was brilliant, you're going to miss it now

Kemi's Dad

Look Kemi, I've got no time now for shooting stars, I have
to get my theory on this stuff, finished by tomorrow

Kemi

Oh Dad! You're such a bore

Kemi's Dad

Kemi we will have another night to go looking
at stars, I promise you, when we fly out to
Canada for my convention tomorrow

Kemi

Tomorrow, Tomorrow, always tomorrow, Canada!
Oh! Boy, can't wait to see Niagara Falls

Ext: As the stars in the sky begin to move in their gravitational orbit above the Earth, still Papiosa chooses to dwell in the nothingness about him, within the midst between the sun and the moon, where the earth hands up all those who have lived and all those she has forgotten, and this is where we find him, watching all that which is born and all that is which is give up to the higher realms.

Peace held its' place and the stars shone all the more brightly between the sun and the moon, but on the earth far across the sea as an ocean liner cruiser was now well and truly underway all the passengers were busy with excitement in themselves as the ship was about to take them on a long and awaited adventure, a women appears on deck standing looking overboard at the endless picture of sea, and tranquility unaware of a male passenger who was observing her.

Davit

Here we are for the first time stowaways on board a
ship set sail for paradise, I always thought I could
just leave it all behind and see the world as time
goes by, you know to get a different perspective on
things, or maybe just to forget for a little while

Miss Felder

Stowaways I beg your pardon, do you think it's' alright
to just come waltzing up to someone, as if you knew them
and start rambling on about paradise, can't you see I'm
taking in the view, I mean really where are your manners
or did you cast them ashore when you came aboard?

Davit

Well Lady, I didn't see any competition around here,
and anyway you looked quite a picture standing there
on the deck, and it struck me as a bit odd, that you
were looking out there across the ocean, I couldn't
have imagined anything more beautiful and perfect

Miss Felder

Look Romeo Romantic, I don't know who the hell
you think you are or what you're doing aboard this
ship but can you kindly do it somewhere else

Davit

It's a boat and by the way, the name is Davit if you please,
listen lady I didn't mean to disturb or upset you in any
way, I just came up on deck to catch a view, just like
you, I wasn't trying to proposition you in anyway, please
accept my apology and let's start again as friends

Miss Felder

Apology accepted now go and bother someone
else and leave me alone with my thoughts

Davit

Leave, and where exactly do you expect me to go?

Miss Felder

Try the other side of this ship or boat, or go
bother the Captain, look here he comes now

**Ext: During Miss Felder's and Davit's conversation, the Captain
makes his presence known.**

Davit

Captain, just the man I've been hoping
to meet and how are you?

Captain

Fine, just fine and you Sir, I didn't catch your name?

Davit

Davit, just Davit

Captain

Well it's a pleasure to have you aboard this vessel
and I hope that you've enjoyed the company of meeting
Miss Felder, we provide a very effective service all
above board, so please feel free to make use of all
the amenities, that means you too Miss Felder

Miss Felder

Are there any lighthouses around this area Captain?

Captain

Lighthouses, that's absolutely ridiculous Miss Felder,
you must be mistaken, and we are miles away from land or
any island or inland port, why do you ask Miss Felder?

Miss Felder

Well what's that light over there I see in the distance, it's
getting larger and larger and closer and closer I do believe?

Captain

Oh that's just probably another ship

Davit

Or a reflection of the sunlight on the water

Ext: As Miss Felder, Davit and the Captain stood on the upper deck of the Boat discussing on what the mysterious light may be, that she had seen, elsewhere Neal's train was steadily heading towards the big city, whilst Kemi and her father were now in mid-flight heading for Canada, the pleasure cruiser with all its' passengers was now well and truly underway but between the heavens and the earth something mysterious was about to take place. Now it may well be divine intervention or it may well be that they were all about to make their very first entry into the realms, because somewhere within space and time they were about to journey and experience something that many would call a process of duality or a paradox that questions everything natural concerning our existence.

1ˢᵗ Mate

Captain, sorry to disturb you Sir, but there's something fast approaching in this direction, our monitors picked up on it just now Sir

Captain

Well, what was its last position?

1ˢᵗ Mate

About a mile sir, South East

Captain

Well if you excuse me Miss Felder, Davit, I'm afraid I'm needed in the control room

1ˢᵗ Mate

Its' gone Captain Sir, its' just disappeared, it was there a moment ago I swear it

Captain

And now nothing, nothing registering on the monitor

1ˢᵗ Mate

No Sir, nothing Sir

Captain

Well that's a bit odd, I thought it was a couples of mile
from here, maybe Miss Felder's ship took another direction

1ˢᵗ Mate

I sense something Captain, something strange, like
a feeling or a sensation but I don't know what it
is, its' all a bit odd and unexplainable, don't
you think, like a presence of something

Captain

Yes, I am also aware, some sort of a chill in the air,
its' very strange, I've been sailing these waters for
thirty years and never felt a force like this

Ext: Just then a sudden flash of bright light appeared

Captain

Great God of Jupiter man steer clear of it man,
throttle off, and bring this vessel to a halt man

1ˢᵗ Mate

Its' too bright Captain I can't see a thing

Captain

I can't get the boat out of the way in time

1ˢᵗ Mate

Well have to go through it Captain,
it's too late to turn around

Captain

Then steer us through it, full throttle, go through
it man, if that's not the brightest light I've seen
I would mistake it for the sun itself, whatever
energy or forces are at work here God help us

Ext: Just then Papiosa appeared from within the light.

Papiosa

Your guide knows you by your innermost need, will
and comfort, and will lead you by your love into
this place of stillness, peace and calm

Int: And so it was as the ship entered into the light, as to did the trains and airplanes which had come to arrive at this place in time, the passengers began to depart their vessels as they stood in astonishment, and marveled as this majestic place, as the way had opened up to the first depth and the people gathered together to try to make sense of what had overcome them, as a stranger walked amongst them with a new sense of being and his name is simply Papiosa.

ANGEL BABIES

THE GOLDEN DAWN

Ext: Upon Papiosa's return to the ruins of oblivion he was chastened by the winds as a storm was brewing amidst the chaos and confusion of darkening clouds, and flashes of lightning in the skies above.

No one knew how long the waters would flow, if not far beyond the infinite realms of the heavens into Nejeru, but flow they did until everything that remained before somehow seemed like a faint memory of a place that use to be long ago, and as the waters cascaded evermore giving way to the souls that were once kept in their soul cages and all that came before them, were by now given over to a higher source and infinite spiritual power.

What I had once witnessed but now may never come to know and yet all that remained in me was in great anticipation and expectation of an event and happening, which even one as I could not have predicted, but had everything suddenly almost become a temporary imagining of the order, or that a horn had been sounded in the heavens or that somehow something or someone had called them home, or had I by now began to find and recognize my feeling, was of a compulsion, and that I too was being pulled or even directed away from the furthest depths and was now succumbing to a greater will or desire upon my own release and realization that maybe somehow it could be that Angelo, had indeed finally reached the zenith through this ever evolving world of creation within this infinite empyrean, both coming and going in and upon succession, until all that had been written and all that was to be, had by now been fulfilled.

Or even that somehow Pablo the Immortal, who was once removed at my demand from his vantage point of being the appointed and ever watchful guardian of Hark himself, the herald Angel, had somehow learnt of a new destiny, through how own selfless act of transcendence to reach me aborne the earthly plains and was by now destined to inspire a source beyond his own revelation through this wisdom of understanding in both purity and light, giving clarity to indeed guide each and every one of us back to our everlasting place of birth, reconciling each one with his or her past and present deeds played upon this ethereal and spiritual world, a kind of Nejeru summoning.

And so even within my own deliberations and questioning knowing soon my time had soon come to be redeemed and fulfilled as had my obligation to serve, had by now come to expire, even as I have heard many words and phrases spoken with patience and hastened by love, as I have seen beyond the horizon of my own eyes in the name of that which I knew only too well, as some may call it the Golden dawn, was soon to beckon me toward my own end, or even until someone would come and alleviate me from my own undoing and the religious constructs which have held and shaped me for so long, but first I must return to the lost souls of oblivion, to fulfill this one last final act of obligation to myself.

Ext: Sitting among the forlorn and forgotten souls of oblivion amongst the shattered ruinous buildings of a ghostly town with a bow in her possession, sits Angel Leoine, a remote sentient and bastion of faith toward the Angel of Justice and the Angel of Mercy, patiently observing the infidels.

Flea
Who are we waiting for again?

Angel Leoine
Silence!

Old Woman
What are we waiting for?

Angel Leoine
Silence!

Spectator
Where are your sisters Bastion, when
will they come to pass us?

Angel Leoine
I said silence!

The Crowd
When will the truth be upon us, I mean truly be known,
what is our fate, if you cannot declare it, then who can?

Angel Leoine
I said silence, now be quiet!

Flea
Who, what, where, when how why, how can we sit in
silence for so long, its' all so painfully boring

Angel Leoine
Wait!

Flea
Why are we waiting?

Angel Leoine
I said wait!

Flea
But who are we waiting for Leoine, tell us?

Angel Leoine
Look!

Old Woman
Where, look where?

Angel Leoine
Here is your judgment

Ext: And there arriving on the distant horizon was Papiosa, drawing nearer and closer with each and every moment and with great momentum.

Papiosa
I am come, but where is Justice, and where is Mercy?

Angel Leoine
You have arrived

Papiosa
And what of Justice and Mercy?

Angel Leoine
They are asleep

Papiosa
For how long?

Angel Leoine
Until your presence was felt

Papiosa
So they are awake?

Angel Leoine
Of course, they are eternal are they not?

Papiosa
I see you have a bow, but why?

Angel Leoine
To smite you if I must

Papiosa

I see you have anticipated my return well

Angel Leoine

Then why did you come?

Papiosa

To see the dawn of course

Angel Leoine

Do not play with my Papiosa

Papiosa

Then I have come to fulfill my judgment

Angel Leoine

But you have no jurisdiction here, surely you must know that

Papiosa

Wherever Papiosa goes, no one can follow and so I do
not need jurisdiction to pass beyond any judgment

Angel Leoine

Then speak your peace and then leave

Papiosa

But Leoine, you know just as I do that
all things must be fulfilled

Angel Leoine

Yes and all things must come to an end, I couldn't
agree more, but in the words of these infidels,
don't you find all of this so painfully boring

Papiosa

What I find, I find in solitude, it bears no
resemblance to anything or anyone one, yes I
know this feeling and it suits me well

Ext: Flea interrupts.

Flea

Papiosa, I see that you've come again to this
forsaken and forgotten place, but why, why are
waiting, are we waiting for you perhaps

Papiosa

Yes! Flea, how can I forget the forgotten and yet
I still see that you've somehow manage to hang on
to that empty cup, a cup of riches no doubt

Ext: Flea laughs to himself.

Old Woman

Ere' he's only come to say goodbye, haven't you papiosa

Papiosa

You and I both know only too well there is no love in goodbye

Old Woman

What do you mean love, Love! Who cares about love, its' as
pointless as it is meaningless, and always a waste of time

Ext: Flea laughs to himself.

Flea

Love, I don't understand

Papiosa

No one understands or knows why flea, **Flea**
Then why did you come?

Papiosa

I came to ask for your freedom

Spectator

Freedom! Freedom from what, how, why, who sent you?

Papiosa

No one

Old Woman

You mean, you came to set us free, for what?

Spectator

For Papiosa's bargaining no doubt

Papiosa

For no one, for yourselves

Angel Leoine

But it is not possible, is it Papiosa?

Papiosa

Oh! But my Bastion, it is

Angel Leoine

I forbid it!

Papiosa

But you cannot

Angel Leoine

Why do you mean I cannot?

Papiosa

Because you do not have the authority

Angel Leoine

But I do, or rather Mercy and Justice have it

Papiosa

Mercy, Justice No! Yes mercy, that's exactly who I
have come to see and then I shall be no more

Flea

Show him Mercy, she'll sooner chop his head off

Int: They all begin to laugh.

Old Woman
He Wants' Mercy, well give it to him then, Mercy! Mercy!
I reckon she'll come to kill him for sure

Papiosa
Be quiet old woman, and do not mock me concerning that which
you do not understand, do you want to become freed or not

Old Woman
Freed! Freed, free, of course I do, but can we trust
you, I mean you are trustworthy aren't you Papiosa

Ext: Papiosa pauses and the looks sincerely at Angel Leoine

Papiosa
I've come to free the forsaken and the forgotten
souls, and to witness the rising of the
Golden Dawn, how say you Angel Leoine?

Angel Leoine
I say you have a redundant position, believe what you want, no
mortal withstanding however blessed has witnessed such a thing

Papiosa
Oh But they have

Angel Leoine
Who?

Papiosa
I cannot tell you that

Angel Leoine
Tell me, tell me now or I'll…

Papiosa
Or you'll what, smite me with your bow, I think not,
now call Mercy so that I can fulfill my obligation both
to her and Justice, so that these so called forgotten

forlorn hopefuls, whom you seem to keep captive if not
hostage for your own personal gratification become freed

**Ext: Suddenly Angel Leoine let out a screeching scream from the
depths of her soul, that echoes and spreads reaching both
far and wide, until in an instant there appeared Angel
Justice and Angel Mercy brandishing a mighty sword in her
hand.**

Papiosa
Mercy! Justice!

Angel of Justice
You should speak when spoken too

Angel of Mercy
What do you want Papiosa?

Papiosa
I want to see the Golden Dawn

Angel of Justice
Impossible!

Papiosa
Not as I understand it

Angel of Mercy
Then you want to die?

Papiosa
Free these infidels, from their judgment

Angel of Justice
What so you can process them in the soul cages, certainly not

Papiosa
No! So they can be set free

Ext: The Angel of Mercy and the Angel of Justice Look puzzled.

Angel of Mercy

Free, free from what, there is only judgment and there is
no freedom, where there is freedom there is a sacrifice

Papiosa

No! Mercy, free them with a gift from the heart, surely you
remember your own heart beating beside your own bosom

Angel of Mercy

But they cannot feel, nor do they know or understand, they
cannot see, nor do they heed or believe, nor have they
witnessed, why should they be free, anyway I find them amusing

Papiosa

That is why Mercy, let them feel freedom, let them
know understanding, let them see, let them heed,
let them find belief in what they choose to witness,
let them contend in their own amusements

Angel of Mercy

No! No I shall not, their mine, they belong to me

Papiosa

Mercy surely you do not regret, even the
beating heart beside your own bosom?

Angel Leoine

Mercy it is true, he is right, let them seek out salvation

Angel of Mercy

Then let them beg for Mercy

**Ext: Just then, the forgotten infidels gathered around Papiosa,
as he exampled each of them by falling to his knees and
coupled his hands, as he urged them all to pray, even as
they all seemed confused and doubtful, and less and less**

willing to speak or utter any words of intent upon their
redemption.

Flea
Why must we pray Papiosa?

Old Woman
We must pray to soften her heart, if she has one

Spectator
Who are we praying for?

Papiosa
We are praying, for deliverance, we must pray for
our childhood dreams, we must pray for love and
for salvation, we must pray for freedom

Ext: And so one by one, each and every lost soul began to pray,
as they never prayed before, and as they're prayers began
to soften Mercy's heart, eventually she lifted up her sword
and wielded it above her head and the suddenly swung it
down striking the ground in front of her, and then the
ground began to rumble and shake beneath them until a
crack began opening up, swallowing everything in its'
path, including that of the forgotten souls but as soon
as they were consumed by the sudden eruption, so too were
their souls released from their afflictions up until their
spirits took flight rising up to realms above and beyond
oblivion.

Ext: Angel Leoine turns to Papiosa.

Angel Leoine
You knew

Papiosa
Yes I knew

Angel Of Mercy
It Is done

Angel of Justice
Yes, It is done

Papiosa
No! Now one more thing

Angel of Mercy
What is it?

Papiosa
I want to see the Golden Dawn

Angel of Mercy
Then ask her yourself

Papiosa
Ask who Mercy?

Angel of Justice
The Bastion, who do you think?

Papiosa
Leoine!

Angel Leoine
I am the Bastion, I am the sentient one of the dawn

Angel Of Mercy
Very well it is done, I bid you farewell

Ext: And in that moment the Angel Of Mercy and the Angel Of Justice were both gone, leaving Papiosa and Angel Leoine to gaze upon the horizon, and Angel Leoine took forth her bow and took aim and fired it into the sky, and as she did so, a magnificent sun filled the skies horizon, overpowering everything in its path

Ext: Papiosa turns to Angel Leoine.

Papiosa

You must go now

Angel Leoine

No I shall stay with you, but tell me, who
told you about the Golden Dawn?

Papiosa

Well let's just say a little Angelo whispered it in my ear

Ext: And as the sun stretched forth its' rays, sending out beams
of light far and wide into the land of oblivion, Papiosa
feared that he would be burned and consumed alive by the
eternal fire and flames of the everlasting and infinite golden
dawn, but in being so brave and forthright, steadfast and
determined to fulfill his obligation in all that Angelo
had set upon his heart and minds imagination, there he sat
watching the rising sun with the presence of Angel Leoine
beside him.

Angel Leoine

Now that you have witnessed the golden dawn Papiosa,
tell me how did you come to learn of this?

Ext: And so Papiosa began to tell Angel Leoine his story of
trial and tribulation from the time of its' inception,
beginning with his dreams as a young boy by his mother's
side, until the famine had taken hold in which many people
of his village did not survive, at which point Papiosa
with much guilt and despair, revealed that maybe in his
being born was the true reason why the famine came , and
that he were somehow responsible for this bad omen which
left so few fighting for survival, inasmuch that the people
reflected it in this by turning their backs on him, as if
he were nothing more than an accursed madman in their
midst, whom no could allow or come to know.

Ext: Papiosa also spoke of his own personal fight for survival,
living off wild berries and shrubs, whilst exploring the
vastness around him, praying each time day by day by the
only remaining stream in the village trying to catch and

yield any fish, believing that somehow his prayers had been answered and with each fish he caught, that somehow a soul if not his own had been saved.

Ext: As this point Angel Leoine had become happy and aroused.

Angel Leoine

Tell me Papiosa, do you not find it strange if not peculiar that you amongst many should escape your fate and not perish by the famine, or that by a simple prayer, you should find a little comfort and food for thought, by the only remaining stream in your village, but tell me more, I want to know everything in your heart and your minds imagination, tell me, what do you know and what you can remember.

Ext: And so Papiosa sat and reflected for a while, and then he began by revealing to Angel Leoine his first encounter with the one he came to call Angelo, and how every night he was tormented every night whenever Angelo came to call, and how every night in his dreams he would die before being called forth into his own resurrection and awakening, and every night dying, and every morning living, until that fateful moment of his vision and his ascension into the realm he came to know as empyrean.

Ext: And now that Angel Leoine had learnt of his trials and tribulations and the coming forth of the one she had anticipated and come to know as Papiosa, she began by explaining how all things were meant to be.

Angel Leoine

When you dreamt, you stood in the doorway of Eden, this was the beginning of your journey and then when you thought you had died, you did not but you were taken up into the several worlds, and then in this world you were given a gift, and if put to good use would become the key to your freedom and salvation, but tell me Papiosa, if it were possible to turn back the hands of time, and for you to be reconciled with your mortal soul, tell me what would you choose.

Ext: At this point Papiosa became confused.

Papiosa

But is this possible, how can it be when I Papiosa,
am here with you in the presence of the Bastion

Angel Leoine

Anything is possible Papiosa, do you not remember
that it was your spirit and not your mortal body
which was taken up into the several worlds, if you
dream deep enough, you shall see that you are still
asleep, where the one called Angelo left you.

Papiosa

Where, where do I sleep?

Angel Leoine

There on the ground at the foot of the
four sided valley, protected by me.

Papiosa

But we are in oblivion, are we not

Angel Leoine

Oblivion is no more, you saw is swept aside and
cast out with your own eyes, did you not

Papiosa

Yes I did

Angel Leoine

So now tell me, if you could go home right now, would
you choose for me to awaken you in the Tetra Valley

Ext: **For a moment Papiosa became still and peaceful and then he
looked toward the Bastion Leoine.**

Papiosa

No! I have had enough of dying and living in
one almighty breath, and I have no need to see
the things of places I wish to forget

Ext: Suddenly Angel Leoine became agitated and angry, and instantly flew to her feet in fury.

Angel Leoine

What do you mean forget! Then what else is there, if not for the past, there is no future, what did you expect that you could sow and reap nothing

Ext: Then Papiosa in his own affliction and aggression shouted

Papiosa

There is nothing!

Angel Leoine

Then I should kill you now! To show you that killing goes on forever, don't you see that this is all there is, only nothing can beget nothing, and therefore nothing can exist, and this is a fallacy to believe otherwise

Papiosa

But people come and go

Angel Leoine

Yes they do, all things must come to pass, but there is never nothing, can you not understand, that we are what we are, an Angel and a mortal alike.

Papiosa

But you are an Angel and a sentient being, and I am a mere mortal man, of flesh and blood.

Angel Leoine

Do you not see Papiosa, that you have the advantage over me?

Papiosa

But how?

Angel Leoine

Because you are blessed and you can die if you don't choose to live, but I am forever more, coming and

going at your will and discretion, its' not fair that
you should possess this power over I, I who have never
loved nor known love, in the way that you have.

Papiosa

But I don't understand, how can you envy me,
when it is I that should envy you.

Angel Leoine

Nay Papiosa, it is not envy of which I speak, it is love.

**Ext: And they both fell silent for a little while, until Angel
Leoine spoke**

Angel Leoine

You are a traitor

Papiosa

A traitor, why, why do you now accuse
me for what I have not done

Angel Leoine

You have betrayed humanity, if you believe in nothing,
then your words are useless and mean nothing

Papiosa

No! My Bastion, do not condemn me, did I not urge
Mercy to free the outcast and forgotten

Angel Leoine

You did, but you did it for nothing, you are their jailor,
and now they shall become nothing, having no place to go

Papiosa

But how, why do you say this Bastion

Angel Leoine

Because it is true, and because you do not possess the
might, and the imagination to guide them home.

223

Papiosa

But there is no hope and there is no home,
there is only suffering and dying.

Angel Leoine

Then this shall be your legacy

Papiosa

Then I have failed to find truth in resolve

Angel Leoine

And I have failed to find triumph in love

Papiosa

What do you mean, an Angel cannot fail, can
they, tell me Bastion is this true?

Angel Leoine

It is true that I have failed you, inasmuch that I love
you, and I desire to live and die beside you if need be

Papiosa

But how can this be Bastion?

Angel Leoine

It can be if you desire it

Papiosa

But in a million breaths, if it were
possible, then yes I would say yes

Angel Leoine

Then it is done, one day we shall eat fish together by
the stream you spoke off, and we shall save every mortal
soul if not our own, come I want to show you something

Papiosa

What is it this time?

Angel Leoine
Have faith in me Papiosa, for I want
to show you the golden dawn

Papiosa
But I thought…

Angel Leoine
You thought, but you did not see

Ext: And Angel Leoine plucked her bow and shot a flaming arrow into the overpowering Sun, and it was done, finally everything remaining in its path was swallowed up until there was nothing other than the shadow of heat across the plains, with the sun now setting over the horizon.

Ext: Now Imagine being suspended high in flight over the Earth and below the heavens above, looking both up toward the stratosphere and down toward the earthly plains and horizons below, whilst having the scope and the capacity to gaze all around you, while taking in the view with each and every breath, in every moment and thought, realizing that time itself was unfolding before you, revealing in your awakening senses, each and every soul that you may ever have transcended or encountered within your lifetime, almost searching and seeking where to fly to next upon this heavenly journey, in and amongst the clouds in the skyline, drifting and sailing along, as if being ferried like timeless memories on a voyage within an infinite spirit, sailing towards the light, thinking of where to descend to next, or simply in anticipation upon the event of readiness to begin your descent, to find what might be your sanctuary or resting place once this flight had cease to take place, and once this Nejeru had called out to you from afar, somehow knowingly you felt that you had arrived and entered into the enlightening realms of the Tetra valley.

Ext: And there one by one, they all began to assemble in the Tetra Valley, where the sleeping body of Papiosa lay, and as the multitudes gathered, a voice could be heard in and amongst the gathering crowd, it was Leoine

Angel Leoine
Let me through, I want to be the first to wake him

Ext: And as Angel Leoine approached Papiosa's body lying on the ground, she outstretched her mortal hand to touch his resting body as she whispered into his ear

Angel Leoine
Papiosa, wake up, it's me, Leoine

Ext: And as Papiosa had arisen, Leoine greeted him with a warm and beautiful smile, there in front of him she stood, along with the entire multitudes and the household of heaven. Welcome

REFERENCE

Edward Tyler (1832 – 1917)

A Soul – Anima R. R. Marett (1866 – 1943)

A Soul – Animism / Animatism North American **Algonquian Indians**

A Soul – Otahchuk

Tetra Valley-(Fictional Place)

The Doctrine of - **(Samsara)**

a former life influences the present one Jiva- (**Hindu** term for the personal Soul or being)

Cavea - (Cage)

Kali Ma - (**Hindu Supreme Goddess** or **Black Earth Mother**)

Mercidiah - (Fictional Earth Mother)

Josephine - (Younger Fictional Earth Mother)

Papiosa - (Fictional Character Depicting Good and Evil)

Men Shen - (**Taoist Interpretation meaning / Guardians of the Door**)

Hark the Herald - (The Listening Angel)

Simeon - (The Protecting Angel)

Pablo - (The Eternal Angel)

Ophlyn - (The Fallen Angel)

Ruen - (The Avenging Angel)

Stefan - (The Angel Of Love)

Angel Leoine - (Bastion & Sentient)

Angel of Justice - (figuratively)

Angel of Mercy - (figuratively)

Nejeru - (New Jerusalem)

Golden Dawn - (The Future)

FINALE

Angelus Domini

A **Tao.House** Product /**AngelBabies**

INSPIRIT ★ ASPIRE ★ ESPRIT ★ INSPIRE

Valentine Fountain of Love Ministry

*Info contact***:** tao.house@live.co.uk